FATED FAMILIAR

A NINE LIVES MAGIC MYSTERY

DANIELLE GARRETT

Big Ghosts Don't Cry

Diamonds are a Ghost's Best Friend

Ghosts Just Wanna Have Fun

Bad Ghosts Club

Mean Ghosts

SUGAR SHACK WITCH MYSTERIES

Sprinkles and Sea Serpents

Grimoires and Gingerbread

Mermaids and Meringue

Sugar Cookies and Sirens

Hexes and Honey Buns

Leprechauns and Lemon Bars

Frosting and Fairies

Candy Apples and Clairvoyants

NINE LIVES MAGIC MYSTERIES

Witchy Whiskers

Hexed Hiss-tory

Cursed Claws

Purr-fect Potions

Furry Fortunes

Talisman Tails

Stray Spells

Mystic Meow

Catnip Charms

Yuletide Yowl

Paw-ful Premonition

Growling Grimoire

Fated Familiar

MAGIC INN MYSTERIES

Witches in the Kitchen

Fairies in the Foyer

Ghosts in the Garden

HAVEN PARANORMAL ROMANCES

Once Upon a Hallow's Eve

A TOUCH OF MAGIC MYSTERIES

Cupid in a Bottle

Newly Wed and Slightly Dead

Couture and Curses

Wedding Bells and Deadly Spells

"I've been skewered! Maimed! Brutalized!"

Scowling, I flipped the rearview mirror down to witness Selene flopping against the backseat like a freshly caught trout.

"Disfigured!" she added, her voice pitching ever higher as she roiled.

"Will you knock it off already? You were microchipped, not skinned alive."

"Permanently scarred!" she replied, no less hysterical than before.

I rolled my eyes. "I saw the needle, Selene. It wasn't *that* big. The whole thing would have taken two seconds if not for your carrying on. And it certainly didn't warrant terrorizing all the pets in the waiting room on the way out. Telling them to get out while they still could."

"Hopefully some of them heeded my warning and made a break for it before it was too late!"

I sighed and readjusted the mirror. The stoplight was still glaring red. "It's for your own good."

"Uh huh, sure," Selene scoffed. "Just admit it, you're a sadist."

"Oh, for the love of Merlin! If you need to blame someone, you'll need one of these—" I tapped the rearview mirror. "You have a history of not following instructions—especially the kind that involve words like 'stay here' and 'keep quiet' and 'no, we can't go look at that fish market over there.'"

"So, because I can think independently, I needed a good shanking? Is that what you're saying?"

"A shanking?" I rolled my eyes a second time.

"The needle was as big as your pinky finger!"

"It absolutely was not." I rubbed the bridge of my nose. All the eye-rolling was threatening to give me a headache. "For the last time, we're going to be a long way from home, and if you wander off and wind up somewhere you're not supposed to be, we now have an easy way to get you back safe and sound, and without blowing our magical cover."

Selene whipped her tail hard enough to make it thump against the backseat. "You make it sound like this will be my first time out in the non-magical world. Like I'm some kind of wide-eyed Pollyanna type without an ounce of street smarts. It's insulting! And now, to make matters worse, you've *branded* me for all of eternity!"

"You haven't been branded."

"I had a number assigned to me, Cora. It's degrading!"

"It's for your protection. The chip is smaller than a grain of rice. It's not like I shaved off your fur and tattooed my name and phone number across your forehead."

"Not yet, anyway," Selene muttered.

At least she'd stopped writhing about.

For now.

All told, the trip to Winterspell's vet clinic had been a moderate success. Dr. Kiki had treated Selene in the past for minor illnesses and knew exactly what type of patient the ten-pound wrecking ball on paws could be. Fortunately, she had spent two decades with the Arcane Order, treating magical creatures, before settling down in the small town to treat dogs, cats, and the occasional wannabe sabertooth tiger. She had experience in spades when it came to unusual patients.

The light changed to green and I rolled into the intersection. "You can call me paranoid if it makes you feel better, but this is for everyone's peace of mind, all right? If you get lost, now a local vet or rescue will instantly be able to look up my phone number and email address and get you back to me. And Aunt Lavender is listed as the backup contact, just in case."

"Oh, good. That ought to help. She lost her phone for three days last week. Want to know where it was?"

I cringed.

"In the blender, Cora. It was in the blender, which she'd put away in the closet, on the top shelf."

"Why was it—" I stopped myself, pinching my lips tight against a myriad of follow-up questions. "I'll see if they can add Mom, too," I quickly added.

Selene made a grunting noise that signaled her dissent was ongoing, but she dropped it. As much as she loved to complain and carry on, she also knew that she was lucky I'd agreed to tag along on my aunt's trip-slash-quest. If not for her, I'd be spending my October in Winterspell, cozy and happy, wearing knit sweaters and watching the leaves fall and trying to keep up with the near-rabid demand for pumpkin spice candles.

Speaking of which...

My gaze darted to the screen on the dashboard, and I winced. It was already four o'clock. "I think we'll have time to get one batch going before we need to get to Mom's," I said.

"Oh, goodie," Selene groaned. "Just when I'd stopped smelling pumpkin and cloves every time I bathed."

"I could give you a proper bath in the sink if you'd like," I teased, flicking a glance at the rearview mirror to gauge her reaction. "Some water and soap might do you wonders."

Selene stood in the center of the backseat, blue eyes wide with abject horror. "You wouldn't dare!"

I smiled. "I was only trying to help."

Selene hissed.

I chuckled and turned onto our street.

FORTY-EIGHT PUMPKIN SPICE–SCENTED candles later, Selene, Clint, and I bid goodbye to Pippin—well, Clint and I said goodbye to the dog—and headed across town to my mom's house for our usual family dinner. Tonight was a bit special, as it was also our sendoff meal, and the moment we stepped inside, I could already tell Mom had outdone herself. The scent of herbs and fresh-baked bread, promising a mouth-watering meal, enveloped us as we shrugged out of our jackets and shoes.

My twin nieces, Ruby and Emme, sat in front of the TV, their angelic faces a little too close to the screen as they sang along with what appeared to be some variety of princess movie, while their little brother, Pierce, marched around them, clanging together two saucepan lids and giggling wildly at the noise. Fortunately, the lids were made of plastic, from the play kitchen Mom had set up a few months ago.

The toddler turned at the sound of the door closing,

and the banging became more frantic as a wide grin spread over his cherubic face. Clint chuckled and bent to scoop the boy up as he lurched toward us. "Hey, champ. You working on your drumming skills?"

I pressed a kiss to the boy's sticky cheek as he wriggled in Clint's arms. "I'm sure your mommy and daddy just *love* that."

As if on cue, my brother, Evan, appeared in the wide arched doorway separating the living room from the kitchen and dining room. He wore a blue-gray flannel with a white crew neck t-shirt underneath, and looked a little bedraggled, while maintaining an easygoing smile. "Oh, yes. And if Aunt Cora and Uncle Clint think they'd be really cute come December and surprise him with a drum kit, I'll remind them that payback can be a real—" He stopped short and cut a sidelong glance to where his daughters sat.

"Witch?" I offered with a grin.

Evan laughed. "Something like that, yes."

Pierce giggled and banged the plastic pot lids together for good measure.

Selene darted inside and made a show of flicking her paws. "Lilac, when are you going to get a new layer of gravel out there? I found another puddle between the pavers!"

Clint groaned and set Pierce down. "Give it a rest, Selene. Unless you're volunteering to come do landscape work in your spare time."

"What spare time?" Selene fired back, her eyes

narrowing in Clint's direction. "As soon as we're back from this harebrained quest, I'm going to reopen Selene's Spells."

I blinked. "Wait, what?"

Selene lifted her chin and stomped on the entryway mat, ridding her delicate toe beans of any lingering moisture. "You heard me. I'll have time to get in on the Christmas rush. And if Walter thinks he can deny me a booth at the market this year, after that mess he made last winter—well, he'll have another think coming!"

Clint and I exchanged a look, and it was immediately clear that neither of us knew quite where to start.

Selene didn't wait around for us to raise our first objection, instead following her nose into the kitchen.

Evan leaned against the doorway, his grin bordering on Cheshire as he looked at Clint. "What are you going to do with yourself while Cora and Selene are gone?"

Clint smiled and wrapped an arm around my waist. "I'll be sitting by the phone, waiting for every call and text, of course."

I patted his stomach with the back of my hand. "Oh, come off it. You and Pippin are going to be living like a couple of carefree bachelors and loving every minute."

Evan laughed. "We're still on for our pickup game next Thursday, right?"

Clint nodded. "Absolutely."

"Good man."

From the kitchen, my sister-in-law's voice called

out Evan's name, and he pushed away from the door-frame. "Speaking of the old ball-and-chain," he teased.

I snorted. "Careful, Evan, if she hears you say that, you might find yourself actually living the bachelor life."

Evan disappeared into the kitchen, and we said hello to the girls, both of whom were so engrossed with the movie they barely offered more than a mumbled reply. Clint settled onto the couch and pulled out his phone, undoubtedly checking work emails. Since I'd shut down the idea of opening a third location of my candle shop, Wicked Wicks, he'd started looking into consulting work, and so far, had two local clients who wanted his help with expanding their businesses into the greater magical world beyond Winterspell's borders.

Smiling, I padded on socked feet to the kitchen, my stomach rumbling as the scent of garlic and roast chicken grew even stronger.

"Hi, honey," Mom called from the stove. Cheyanne glanced up from her work, carving the bird, and Selene seized the opportunity to swipe one of the drumsticks off the platter to my sister-in-law's right.

"Selene!" I exclaimed, though it was no use as the sound of maniacal laughter and skidding paws echoed from down the back hallway.

Cheyanne growled in frustration. "I took my eyes off it for *one* second!"

I winced. "I'm sorry."

Mom dipped a spoon into the saucepan and clucked her tongue. "If she'd waited another minute, I would have told her I'd bought some of that overpriced smoked salmon dip she always goes on about. Oh well. I guess she doesn't need any of it now, seeing as she's already had herself a treat." Mom winked at me, and I laughed.

"That ought to teach her."

Cheyanne scoffed and went back to carving up the chicken breast. "Mission impossible, if you ask me."

The back door opened and Evan came inside. He stomped his shoes off on the mat before kicking out of them. "Cans are at the curb," he told Mom.

"Thank you, dear."

"Is Aunt Lavender on her way?" I asked.

"Oh, I expect she'll be here any minute," Mom replied breezily. "I've got a few more things to do, then we'll get these potatoes out of the oven. I'm just waiting for the last of the cheese to melt."

Smiling, I looked at the prepared dishes lined up on the counter. A large bowl of fruit salad sat beside a mixed green salad topped with veggies and seeds and dried cranberries. Garlic rolls were wrapped in aluminum foil, already browned to golden perfection. A platter with cut vegetables and hummus sat beside a plate with a cheese ball and assortment of crackers, both of which had already been sampled.

"You've outdone yourself, as always," I said. "Anything I can do to help?"

"Why don't you and Clint finish setting the table. Evan got started before I sent him out on trash duty."

Evan tipped an invisible cap.

"On it!"

I was just about finished with the table when the front door opened, and I peeked around the corner to find my aunt and her familiar, a black-and-white cat. Checkers shook his medium-length coat off like a dog —something Selene would surely not approve of— before he cocked his head toward the TV and raced over to join my nieces and nephew. "Oh, this is my favorite part!" the cat exclaimed.

Aunt Lavender smiled after her familiar, then met my gaze. "Evening, Cora! Are you all set for our adventure?"

Selene came out to the living room, wearing a cat-that-ate-the-entire-stolen-drumstick grin. "Cora, there's a bit of a mess in the hallway you might want to see to."

I frowned. "Let me guess, it involves a chicken bone and some gristle bits?"

She flashed her teeth in a feline grin.

"Honestly, cat—"

"Hey, I'd say I earned it! After you had me bagged and tagged like some kind of sick hunting trophy!"

Checkers padded over and stood at Aunt Lavender's side.

"Selene was microchipped at the vet," I explained.

Checkers swished his fluffy tail. "Oh, come on, Selene. It's not that bad."

Selene's blue eyes narrowed to icy slits. "Not that bad?"

"The cat nurse gave me liver-flavored pate when I got mine!" Selene continued to glower and Checkers laughed. "You're being a big kitten."

Aunt Lavender laughed behind her hand as the two cats squared off. "Come now, Checkers, let's go see what Lilac has been up to. Whatever it is, it smells divine!"

Selene hissed as Checkers passed by her.

I nudged her with the side of my foot. "Be nice, Selene."

My familiar continued glowering at the oblivious Checkers. "All right, but if we hit rough waters, don't be surprised if that one winds up going overboard."

I rolled my eyes but made a mental note to keep tabs on the hapless cat during any and all water travel.

Considering our track record, it was likely foolish to assume our Grecian adventure would go off without a hitch, but I drew the line at sabotage. So far as it was up to me, we'd all be back in Winterspell, safe and intact, just in time for Halloween.

2

*I*n the weeks leading up to our departure, I'd imagined a grand arrival to the island of Santorini. Not that it was hard to daydream about a place so beautiful. I envisioned the white, sand-blasted homes with the blue roofs perched over the glittering Aegean Sea.

Unfortunately, the reality was a letdown. Thanks to two long travel days, riddled with delays and problems —and one intensely cranky cat—we arrived in Santorini well after nightfall and missed seeing the picturesque aerial view altogether.

By the time we departed the airport, all any of us wanted was a comfortable bed and a good night of sleep. Unfortunately, that was also not in the cards. Aunt Lavender maintained she'd booked three separate rooms and insisted there must be some sort of glitch, but I had my doubts. In any case, the three ocean-view rooms became one room with two beds and the promise of a rollaway cot.

"I should have brought that silencer thing Leanna brought to the wedding," I growled as we shuffled into our makeshift accommodations.

"No one heard me talk," Selene replied, her tone every bit as sour as my own.

"Talk? No. But I doubt there's anyone on this entire island who didn't hear you yowling in a suspiciously human manner," I snapped as I set the cat carrier down a little too roughly.

"We made it, and that's all that matters," Mom said, though even her sunny-side-up tone was starting to grow thin.

Aunt Lavender set down the hard plastic pet carrier containing Checkers, then stretched her arms overhead before leaning over to free her familiar.

"People were already looking at us like we were nuts," I added. "Flying around the Greek isles with a couple of cats. Then you had to go and have a conniption fit in the lobby in the middle of the night!" I shook my head, but instantly regretted it as my headache throbbed in protest. "Mother of Merlin."

Mom dragged her suitcase across the floor, one of its wheels spinning errantly on the thin carpet. "I should have asked if they offer room service. The idea of going anywhere right now makes my eye twitch."

Checkers hopped onto one of the matching queen-size beds. "This place looks okay to me," he concluded.

"Considering you grew up under a dumpster, that's not exactly reassuring," Selene muttered, her paws digging at the plastic. "Why isn't my magic working on this door?!"

Pink sparks filtered through the metal grate across the front, but the door remained in place.

Aunt Lavender quirked a smile over her shoulder. "Told you it would work."

"You did this?! You old hag, first the micro—"

I set the carrier down a little harder than intended. "Say microchip *one* more time, Selene, I dare you."

Checkers' eyes went wide. "Ooooo."

"Stay out of it, runt!" Selene growled, before another blast of magic burst through.

"Hey, I'm bigger than you!"

I leaned over and glared through the bars. "Stop thrashing and I'll let you out. And no more yowling. We talked about this, Selene."

"You three were letting those front desk people walk all over you! If you'd let me handle it, we'd be holding the key to the presidential suite by now!"

I stopped short of releasing the latch. "No ... we'd be in a police station, using our one phone call to beg Warden Quinton to send someone to rescue us and wipe everyone's memories."

Selene's tail *thwapped* against the sides of the carrier. Reluctantly, I steeled myself and released the latch. The door opened and Selene stalked out, her tail aloft and slightly fluffier looking than usual.

Oh boy. That was never a good sign.

"Listen," I said, hoping to cut off her next complaint at the pass, "it's been a long day. We're all tired and hungry. Let's get cleaned up and order some room service. Things will all look better in the morning."

"I, for one, will feel better once the airplane air is rinsed out of my hair," Mom said with a cheerful smile. "Anyone mind if I hop in the shower first?"

Selene jumped onto the low windowsill and wriggled her whiskered face between the heavy curtains. "Seems dangerous. Your bone density isn't what it used to be, Lilac."

Mom's smile soured. Beside her, Aunt Lavender jolted. "Oh. That reminds me, did I remember to pack my calcium chews?"

"They're in the tote with the autumnal floral print," Checkers said. "Middle pocket."

I bit my tongue and managed to stop short of asking Selene why she couldn't be helpful like Checkers. After all, the day had been stressful enough, we didn't need to cap it off with a homicide.

THINGS DID, in fact, look better in the morning. Of course, in a place as beautiful as Santorini, that wasn't hard. The morning sun painted the island in hues of gold and azure, a stark contrast to the chaotic darkness of our arrival. We'd slept in as much as we could before wandering down to a quaint waterfront café, where we could enjoy the view and drink copious amounts of espresso.

"Now this is more like it." Mom sighed contentedly, cradling a tiny white cup in her hands.

With a relaxed smile, I snaked a hand toward the plate of delicate pastries between us and snagged a baklava. "Agreed!"

Aunt Lavender, already on her second cup of tea, leaned back in her chair with a dreamy expression. "Isn't it marvelous? The island is steeped in such wonderful history. It's been too many years since I've been back."

The iconic, blue-domed structures dotted the cliff-side, their vibrant color mirroring the endless expanse of the cerulean waters below. Fishing boats bobbed gently in the harbor, their painted hulls adding splashes of color to the picturesque scene.

As much as I loved autumn in Winterspell, it was hard to miss it while surrounded by such beauty. "It really is stunning," I added with a dreamy smile. "The pictures don't do it justice."

"I'm just glad it's not crawling with tourists," Selene interjected, her tail flicking lazily as she basked in the swath of sunlight stretching across the stone patio.

"Selene!" I hissed, whipping around to scan the street in either direction. "Ix-nay on the alking-tay!"

Checkers, who had been contentedly lapping up some honey-drizzled yogurt, perked his ears. "Huh?"

"Not you, too," I groaned.

Aunt Lavender chuckled, reaching over to scratch behind his ears. "No one is watching, Cora."

"Yet," I muttered as I tore off a piece of baklava.

Selene snickered under her breath but fell silent as our server swept over to deliver our full breakfast order. From there, I kept her mouth busy with oodles of baked sardines.

It would all become a bit less stressful once we were out on the water. Aunt Lavender was convinced she had discovered the exact coordinates of the Lost City of Atlantis, and had chartered a boat to take us out so she could have a look. Mom had surprised everyone by taking scuba diving classes at the tail end of summer, and was prepared to go poke around with her sister.

Personally, I'd opted to stay above the waves and planned to keep an eye on Checkers and Selene.

The meal was nearing its conclusion when Aunt Lavender's watch beeped. She tapped the button on the side to silence it and flashed an eager grin around the table. "That's our cue! The boat should be ready for us."

Mom fished some bills from her wallet—she'd been designated the treasurer of the trip—and Selene gobbled the remaining bites of sardine from her own plate, before nosing around in Checkers' leftovers for good measure. I watched her with a disapproving scowl and finished my espresso.

The walk to the marina was a feast for the senses. The narrow, winding streets were lined with charming shops and cafés, their doors flung open to catch the cool morning breeze. Aunt Lavender led the way, and I did my best to avoid the eyes of the other pedestrians on the street, many of whom looked curiously in our direction. Or, more accurately, in the direction of the two cats who walked with my aunt, one on each side.

As we rounded the final corner, the harbor came back into view. An array of watercraft bobbed and swayed in the water, everything from weathered fishing boats to sleek yachts that probably cost more than my shop grossed in a fiscal year.

Aunt Lavender paused to check her phone before turning and walking down a long dock. She held one hand over her face, shielding her eyes from the morning sun as she scanned the numbered placards. We'd nearly reached the end of the line when she stopped abruptly and pointed at a modest sailboat. "Here we are! The *Mermaid's Pearl*. She's ours for the day."

"*Mermaid's Pearl*, huh?" Selene approached the boat and sniffed. "I suppose this will do."

"Oh, good, now that we have the Selene's seal of approval, we can set sail." I scoffed, then quickly glanced around to make sure no one would overhear.

Selene ignored me and hopped aboard. "Where's the captain?"

Aunt Lavender lifted her chin and smiled, revealing a mischievous glint in her eyes. "You're looking at her!"

My jaw dropped. "You? But ... do you even know how to sail?"

"Oh, Lavender, I'm not sure that's such a good idea," Mom said, sliding a concerned glance in my direction.

Selene snickered from somewhere over the side of the boat.

Aunt Lavender sniffed. "Checkers and I have watched over a dozen hours of tutorials on that tube thing—" She waved vaguely in her familiar's direction.

"YouTube," he interjected quietly.

"Yes, that's it. It doesn't look all that hard. And besides, we have magic!"

Selene's head poked over the side of the boat. "At least there aren't any leaks. No rats, either, though I was hoping for a bit of a snack..."

I frowned. "You *just* ate."

"We're on vacation, Cora. Everyone knows you get hungrier on vacation." She swiveled her gaze to her former guardian. "I suppose a scrawny rat wouldn't make for much of a last meal, though. Perhaps we should go find an ice cream shop before we depart on our final voyage."

Aunt Lavender skewered the cat with a narrowed glare. "Stop being dramatic, Selene." She turned the frosty stare on the rest of us before adding, "We're on an adventure! Or have you already forgotten?"

Selene glowered. "Of the two of us, I'm not the one who is losing their mind."

"You're sure we don't need some kind of permit or, uh, license, Lavender?" Mom asked, her gaze shifting from the boat to the open water beyond.

"We don't need to bother with all that, Lilac. It's a quick out and back again. I paid a man, he told me where to find the boat, it's all sorted."

She really wasn't going to be happy if we didn't end up in jail, was she?

I glanced down at Selene, hoping she might attempt to talk some sense into my aunt. After their years together, she generally knew the right tactic to take in such circumstances. But she wasn't paying attention to either me or her former guardian. Instead, she had poor Checkers—poor, oblivious, sweet-as-powdered-sugar Checkers—in her sights.

"And where were you while these so-called *arrangements* were being made?" she snapped, her tail whipping back and forth.

Checkers blinked and swiveled his head toward Selene, his medium-length fur dancing in the sea breeze. "Huh?"

"Exactly! Lavender, what have I told you about—"

Footsteps sounded behind me, the boards of the dock creaking under the weight of three people and a trio of rolling suitcases. I prodded Selene in the side, which earned me a deadly scowl, but served my purpose in drawing her attention to the fact that we were still in public.

She growled but fell silent.

Aunt Lavender, undeterred, clapped her hands together and beamed. "Who's ready to set sail?"

AMID A FLURRY OF COMPLAINTS, overt skepticism, and general confusion, we somehow managed to navigate the sailboat out of the marina. I'd hoped to be a tad more inconspicuous, but it turns out three women in a sailboat with a pair of cats was something of an attention getter, and our loud squabbling made it impossible to fully slip away unnoticed. I just hoped no one realized the two extra voices, as both Selene and Checkers abandoned the "no talking" rule.

By some goddess's blessing, we got the sail up and pointed in the right direction to catch the morning breeze and sailed until we reached the coordinates Aunt Lavender kept repeating to herself, like a mantra.

"This is it?" I asked, glancing around. The island was still close enough for the shore to be visible, though the marina was a blur on the vast canvas of brilliant blue water.

Aunt Lavender consulted some electronic gadget

she'd packed, then gave a definitive nod. "This is it!" She set down the tool and beamed.

"You two better get to swimming then," Selene said from her place on a long bench seat. "And someone adjust that sail. It's blocking my sun. Cora, what snacks did you bring?"

"We can't just dive in," Aunt Lavender said, though not unkindly. Her eyes sparkled with anticipation as she reached for a thin chain around her neck, pulling it out from beneath her linen blouse. Dangling from the end was an ancient-looking coin. "If it were as simple as all that, anyone would have discovered it by now."

Selene looked up, but gave a lazy thump of her tail. "That's the coin with Amphitrite on the front? Your so-called *key* to Atlantis?"

Aunt Lavender's smile only widened as she lifted the chain from around her neck and ran the pad of her thumb over the face. "Indeed!"

"She's done a lot of reading about it," Checkers assured us.

Selene laid her head back down.

"So, how does it work?" I asked, a little tentative as I looked over at Mom. "A key implies there's some kind of lock."

I scanned the still waters around us once more.

"There must be one somewhere," Aunt Lavender replied.

And then, before any of us could object, she leaned

22

over the side of the boat and dropped the necklace into the crystal-clear water.

For a moment, nothing happened. The coin disappeared beneath the surface with barely a ripple. We all peered over the edge, waiting.

"Well, that was anticlima—" I began, but the words died in my throat.

The water around our boat began to churn, slowly at first, then with increasing speed. A whirlpool formed, growing larger by the second, the once-calm sea now a roaring vortex.

"Lavender!" Mom shouted over the noise. "What's going on?"

But there was no time for answers. The whirlpool expanded, catching our sailboat in its powerful current.

"Oh, what have you done now, you old bat?!" Selene yowled.

Aunt Lavender yelped as the boat pitched wildly to the right and we grabbed onto whatever we could— railings, masts, each other—as the boat began to spin.

The world became a blur of blue and white as we spun faster and faster. The boat tilted precariously, water sloshing over the sides. And then, with a final, mighty pull, the whirlpool sucked us under.

I took one last desperate breath before we plunged beneath the waves, darkness enveloping us as we were pulled into the unknown depths of the Aegean Sea.

3

The world became a blur as the waves pulled us under, but almost as quickly as it began, it seemed to reverse. The pull became a fervent push, and suddenly I was shoved back above the water, like a cork flying from a bottle of celebratory champagne. My body tumbled onto a bank of coarse sand, face first.

Nearby, I could hear the confused groans and mutters of my family as they too were dislodged onto the beach.

The question was *which* beach. As I sat up and spat out the sand from my mouth, I took in our surroundings. The small, crescent-shaped shoreline looked unspoiled and wild, its golden sands giving way to lush vegetation just a few yards inland. Tropical trees and dense undergrowth created a verdant wall, their leaves rustling in the warm breeze.

The white walls and blue rooftops of Santorini

were gone, as were most other signs of civilization, but for a solitary house—well, rather, estate. A magnificent mansion sprawled over a hillside overlooking the sea. Its warm, sandstone-colored walls and red-tiled roof stood in contrast to the lush greenery surrounding it, but the overhangs above its many windows and balconies were draped with flowering vines, as though the island had accepted the home and embraced it as a part of itself. The building was an exquisite example of Mediterranean architecture, with tall windows and graceful arches. A grand staircase led up to the entrance, flanked by rose bushes and more greenery.

"Where … where are we?" Mom's voice broke through my daze.

"I have no idea," I replied, still taking in the surreal scene before us. "Aunt Lavender?"

She sat, slack-jawed, staring up at the stunning estate. Our borrowed boat floated in the near distance. Belly side up, for lack of the proper nautical term.

"Lavender?!" Mom snapped. "What is this? Where are we? Is this—Atlantis?"

My aunt got to her feet with an easy grace that belied her age. "Most certainly not." She frantically looked around the shore. "Checkers?!"

"Here!" a small voice called as the cat emerged from behind a sizeable chunk of twisted driftwood. He paused to shake off, then looked down at himself, his pained expression growing more pitiable.

We were all drenched, our clothing sticking to our

skin and collecting sand as we trudged toward one another.

"Did you know this would happen?" Selene snapped as she tried—and failed—to flick sand off her paws.

"Of course I didn't!" Aunt Lavender replied, her tone every bit as sharp as her former familiar's. "If I did, I think I would have put on my diving equipment ahead of time. Honestly, Selene. You should know better."

Selene paused her miserable bathing efforts to scowl at the woman. "That's rich, coming from you! We could have died!" She paused, blinked, then added, "Well, you all could have died. And then what would I do? Cora made you all the emergency contacts for this tracking device she implanted into my spine!"

I rolled my eyes and wrung out the bottom half of my shirt.

"Someone's coming!" Mom exclaimed, her voice a frantic hiss.

Turning, I followed her gaze to a figure descending the exterior staircase carved into the sand-colored stone of the house. The woman looked quite stately, with a sleek updo of dark hair and a flowing blue dress that matched the hues of the rooftops along Santorini's coast. Ahead of her marched a fluffy black cat, whose nose and tail both pointed into the air with a sense of self-importance I could clock from a hundred yards away.

Mainly because I saw that look every day.

Selene caught it, too, and her hackles—damp as they were—rose along with a growl in the back of her throat.

Mom waved her arms over her head, as though attempting to flag down a search and rescue helicopter. "Please, can you help us?!" she called.

"Lilac, they could be cannibals!" Selene hissed.

I gaped at my familiar. "Oh, for the love of—"

"We just need to flip that little dinghy of yours and get the heck out of here," Selene continued. "Come on, Cora. A little help here."

The woman and cat reached the end of the stairs, and I turned to look back at Selene. She stood staring at the wreckage, the tip of her tail crooked toward it. "What do you expect me to do? My magic isn't strong enough to flip something that big. Especially not with all the water. It's way too much resistance."

"Well, then you'd better put your back into it!" Selene snapped. "You push, I'll handle the magic."

"Oh! I think I see the coin!" Water splashed as Aunt Lavender ran a little ways down the coast. She bent and plucked something from the sand, frowned, and flicked it over her shoulder with a grunt of frustration. "Never mind. It was a fragment of shell."

Selene rolled her eyes, then jabbed a flicker of pink sparks toward the boat to draw my attention back to my assigned task.

"Hello!" Mom called.

I turned my back on Selene—always something of a

dangerous prospect—and went to stand beside Mom as the stranger approached. With a polite, if not slightly frazzled smile, I raised a hand in greeting and began to add my own salutation when the dour-looking woman snapped, "Who are you people and what are you doing here?"

Mom and I flinched.

"That depends on who's asking." Aunt Lavender replied, coming to join us. She folded her arms over her chest and gave the woman a once-over glance.

Mom grimaced and tossed a bit of extra sweetness into her voice as she launched into an explanation. "We're so sorry to disturb you, but we seem to have been caught in … uh, well, a whirlpool, I suppose it was." She looked at me and I offered a quick bob of my head in agreement.

Checkers sat at his guardian's feet and cocked his head to peer up at the woman, his fur hopelessly stuck to the sides of his face. "Are you Amphitrite?"

The woman reared back, as though slapped. "I—I'm sorry—"

Right, so the talking cat bit was fully out of the bag. Excellent.

I exhaled a nervous laugh, but before I could think of a cover story or lie, the cat standing at the woman's side narrowed its yellow-green eyes. "Hm. Well, at least we know they're witches," said a baritone voice. "Who blabbed? I'll bet it was Alexandra? She's always going on about inviting that friend of hers." The cat eyed us in turn with the intensity of an inspector in a high-octane spy thriller.

"We don't know any Alexandra," I stammered.

"Alexandra knows better," the woman said, ignoring me entirely as she glanced down at her feline companion. "And besides, she wouldn't have sent them through the sea door."

The cat's whiskers twitched. "Ah. So one of the nymphs, then. Probably your little pet…"

The woman frowned, though it did nothing to detract from her almost regal beauty. Checkers' question might have sounded a bit left field, but there was a striking resemblance between the woman's features and that of the woman depicted in sculptures and paintings from the region.

"In either case, I say we toss them back into the sea and let Louka deal with it," the cat added before looking up at his presumed guardian with a bored expression and a lazy swish of a fluffy tail.

The woman canted her head to one side, giving the suggestion a moment of consideration.

Selene's still-damp fur did its best to stand on edge as she flashed her teeth. "I'd like to see you try!" A flurry of pink sparks swirled around us, forming a barrier. While it technically was my magic she was borrowing, I couldn't be sure what spell she was cooking up, but knowing her, it would end in disaster —I just wasn't sure which side would take the brunt of it.

I raised a hand. "We don't mean to intrude. Or, uh, trespass. This was all—" I paused and looked back at the capsized sailboat. "A mistake. I … think."

"A mistake?" The woman lifted her strong chin. Up close, I could see streaks of silver in her neatly coiffed hair. Her face had an olive-hued tone and while I imagined she spent a fair bit of time in the sun, her skin had only the faintest of fine lines around her eyes and mouth. If she wore makeup at all, it was extremely subtle, perhaps only to extend the dark lashes framing deep brown eyes. "No. This is not possible. There must have been a coin. There always has to be a coin."

Before we could reply, she raised a hand and made a curling motion with her fingers. The waves seemed to pause, if only for the barest flicker of a moment, and then Aunt Lavender's coin, with the delicate chain still attached, rose from the sea and sailed toward the woman, where it dropped neatly into her palm. Her thin lips pulled back into a cold sneer as she stared down at the coin.

"They punched a hole in it?!" the cat exclaimed, standing up on his hind legs to try and get a better look. When he lowered back to stand on all four paws, he swirled, his tail growing nearly twice its size. "Loukaniko!"

"Calm yourself, Trident," the woman said, though her soured expression remained as she lifted her gaze from the coin to consider us once more. "Tell me where you got this."

It wasn't a question.

The cat stalked to the water's edge. "Where is that blasted serpent?"

I swallowed hard and watched him stalk across the damp sand, my mouth suddenly dry. "I'm sorry— serpent?"

A flicker of movement caught the corner of my eye, and I turned my head just as the waters parted once more. Only this time, instead of a lost coin, a huge serpentine head emerged. Blue and silver, the glossy scales reflecting the golden sunlight, making them shimmer like crystals. Bony fins protruded from the creature's head and brilliant emerald eyes flashed with a hungry gleam.

Selene let out a string of frantic words that I took to be swear words in several different languages, while Checkers looked caught between making a run for it and making a final stand between Aunt Lavender and the creature.

"Finally!" Trident scoffed. "What were you doing? You're supposed to be here, watching for arrivals."

The beast let out a low whine and lowered its head, the eyes looking down at the water that stirred around his massive neck.

"Don't give me that!" the cat chided. "You have a job to do! Especially today!"

"That's enough, Trident," the woman said. She gave us a sharp-eyed glance, but moved toward the serpent. "He was probably off getting something to eat," she added, stretching out a hand. The serpent perked up and pressed his nose into her open palm, like a needy dog. "There's my little sausage."

Trident hissed.

"Little?" I gulped. Each of the creature's eyes was roughly the size of the woman's fist.

Selene sliced a look over to my aunt, her tail lashing violently back and forth. "Exactly what kind of funhouse horror mirror did we just step through, Lavender?"

The woman looked up at the question, though she continued running one hand over the scaled nose of the serpent. "Who gave you the coin?"

"No one gave it to me," Aunt Lavender replied. "I found it, and I would very much like to have it back. We're on a quest for the Lost City, and I believe it to be the key. Now … clearly there's been a bit of a miscalculation here—"

Selene huffed a dry laugh. "Gee, ya think?"

"But my purpose remains the same," Aunt Lavender continued, sparing only the briefest of glowers for her former familiar. "Now, if you'll hand it over, and perhaps help us with the boat, we'll be on our way."

The woman in blue ran her hand down the serpent's nose, then snapped her fingers and pointed out toward the horizon. The serpent lowered its eyes and head, giving the look of a sad hound dog, before it obediently slipped back under the surface and slithered away.

Trident puffed out his chest and watched until the fins vanished.

"I'm afraid that's not how this works," the woman said, turning back toward us. "The magic that allowed you access to this island only opens during specific times. No one will be allowed off the island until the full moon begins to wane."

"What? But that's—"

The woman held up a hand. "There is no use in arguing. I do not make the rules, I can only follow them. As will you."

"But who—who are you? What is this place? Where are we?"

"My name is Althea Zosimos, the eighth of my name, and this is Chrysanthe Island. Home to Athánatos House and host of the Sisterhood of Amphitrite."

Althea did not wait for us to respond before she swept back toward the stately home, the hem of her long blue dress now damp as it trailed over the sand.

The five of us exchanged long, silent glances, then followed the woman.

Selene glanced back at the water. "I don't know what you've gotten us into, but I'd wager you're not getting back whatever deposit you put on that boat, Lavender."

$\mathcal{W}$e followed Althea and Trident up the carved stone staircase. I hadn't yet dumped the water out of my slip-on shoes, and they made a squelching sound with every step. As we climbed, the full grandeur of Athánatos House came into view. Its sandstone walls, tinged golden in the afternoon light, were adorned with climbing vines bearing delicate white flowers. Ornate wrought-iron balconies jutted out from between tall windows on the second floor, marking the rooms. More dangling vines draped with fragrant flowers climbed the wooden pergola over the front entry, and I breathed deeply, trying to commit the scent of the flowers and the sea to memory. The whole scene—mysterious and unsettling as it was—would make for a beautiful candle.

Mom, Aunt Lavender, and I exchanged nervous glances as we reached the double doors leading into the house. Althea opened the pair with a wave of her hand, and Selene padded silently between my ankles, taking the lead. Checkers hurried to catch up with her, but not before giving my aunt a quick glance.

Althea strode into the house, her blue dress flowing behind her like the gentle waves we'd left behind. Trident walked proudly beside her, his fluffy tail held high like a banner. Every so often, he would glance back at us, his chartreuse eyes narrowed with suspicion.

The floor in the entry was tiled with a beautiful mosaic depicting sea creatures and an array of blue hues, all framing the likeness of a woman rising from the sea, her arms outstretched. Amphitrite, I presumed, though her face bore an uncanny resemblance to our hostess.

The floor plan was surprisingly open and revealed a marvel of classical Greek architecture mixed with nautical themes. Marble columns rose to a vaulted ceiling adorned with a fresco depicting an underwater scene—nymphs, fish, and a pair of golden dolphins. A grand staircase curved up to the second floor, its balustrade carved to resemble waves.

My eyes couldn't seem to stay in one place. Everywhere I looked there was some new wonder to behold. A painted vase that looked as though it should be sitting behind thick glass in a museum sat on a circular table, filled with soft pink flowers. Tapestries hung on the wall that veered off to the left, into a hallway. "This is beautiful."

"Thank you," Althea replied, though her tone held no warmth.

Selene flicked the tip of her tail. "Where exactly are we? And why haven't I heard of this so-called 'Sisterhood of Amphitrite' before? And what's with the name? Athánatos?"

Trident stopped short and whirled around, his yellow-green eyes flashing. "You'd do well to mind your manners, *cat*. Athánatos House is a sacred place."

Selene's fur bristled. "Sacred place, huh?" She took a pointed look around the entryway and the living room beyond. "Looks more like one of the hotels in Athens that caters to tourists who want the full Greek experience. You know, columns and mosaics, little lightning bolts on everything, and stuffed grape leaves at every meal. Tell me, do you do the maid service, or is that beneath your oh-so-important station?"

"Why, you insolent little—" Trident began, taking a step towards Selene.

"Enough," Althea said, her voice calm but carrying an undeniable note of authority. "Trident, these are our guests, unexpected as they may be."

The two cats glared at each other, neither backing down. I could feel the tension crackling between them like static electricity.

Aunt Lavender cleared her throat. "It's a lovely home. But, as we said, we didn't intend to come here—"

"Wherever *here* is," Selene added with a scoff.

"We are seventeen miles off the coast of Santorini. The coin allowed you passage through the protective wards that keep the island concealed." Althea gestured toward a set of ornate double doors across the large, sunken living room. "Every member of the Sisterhood has a coin, and it leads them to the passageway."

"You said something about the sea door?" I prompted as we followed her across the expansive room, careful not to take a wrong step on the shallow step down. "And ... uh, nymphs?"

"That's right," Althea said breezily, not looking back.

I waited a beat for her to elaborate, then glanced down at Selene when it became clear she wasn't planning to expound further.

Selene's eyes narrowed.

"We are waiting for one more to join us, but come out and I'll introduce you. Then we will see about finding you a room."

"Surely that won't be necessary," Mom said, her expression knit with concern. "There must be some way to let us leave."

Beside me, Aunt Lavender had fallen uncharacteristically silent as she took her time crossing through the house, her gaze roaming about the various pieces of art and furnishings. Checkers stayed close to her, glancing up every other step, as though waiting for his orders.

"I'm afraid not," Althea said.

"You should just be grateful she's offering you a place to stay," Trident grumbled. "I still think we should let Loukaniko deal with you. He should be earning his keep, if you ask me." The last part was directed to his guardian with a pointed look.

Althea glanced down, but did not argue with her familiar.

"He might be grumpier than you, Selene," Aunt Lavender said from a step behind me.

Trident snapped his head around and glowered.

Selene mirrored his disgruntled expression.

"You said we could leave when the full moon begins to wane," Mom said, undeterred by the conversation swirling around her. "When will that be?"

Althea stopped at the doors, one hand resting on the handle. "In three days' time."

I jolted. "Three days!"

Althea drew in a breath and turned to face us. She stood taller than any of us, though not by much when it came to Aunt Lavender. "Listen, this is not ideal for any of us. You are not meant to be here, but there is nothing I can do to change that now."

Blue and silver sparks buzzed around Trident and his glower intensified. "I don't know about that—"

With a severe frown, Althea snapped her fingers and the sparks vanished. "Trident, why don't you go and speak with Zora. Let her know we'll need an extra room prepared for guests."

Trident looked ready to argue, but when he glanced

up and saw the expression on his guardian's face, he changed his mind and stalked off, muttering to himself.

Althea lifted her chin. "Now, if you'll please follow me." She opened the door and stepped outside.

The deck off the living room was large and surrounded by lush greenery, with a gorgeous ocean view framed by the trees and flowering vines that hung from the pergola covering most of the deck with shade. A large table, with room to seat fourteen people, dominated the center of the space. Several faces turned at our arrival and surprise registered before being replaced by questioning glances in Althea's direction.

A woman with bronzed skin and glossy black hair, cut into a long bob, jumped up from her seat at the head of the table. "Althea?" she asked, clutching an electronic tablet to her chest. She wore a linen shirt that looked casual but expensive, and simple gold jewelry.

"It seems we have some unexpected guests," Althea said with a smile that looked a little too tight.

Whispers and gasps ricocheted around the table.

"What?" the woman at the head of the table said, her gaze darting from us to Althea and back again. "What do you mean? How is that—I mean, they couldn't have—"

"I don't yet know," Althea said, sliding us a sidelong glance. "I thought it best they came and explained it to all of us." She paused and glanced around the table. Aside from the standing woman, there were five other women present, all wearing matching expressions of bewilderment.

"All right," Aunt Lavender said, stepping in line with Mom and me. All eyes swiveled toward her, including Althea's. "My name is Lavender Hearth. This is my sister, Lilac, and my niece, Cora. The black-and-white cat is Checkers, my familiar, and the other one is—"

"The *other one*?!" Selene burst out.

I flinched. This wasn't going to end well.

"How dare you!" Selene continued, her tail flicking wildly back and forth.

"Is Selene," Aunt Lavender continued, ignoring her former familiar's glower and bluster.

"How did you find us?" one of the women asked, while at the same time another demanded, "What do you want?"

Althea held up her hand, displaying the coin pinched between her thumb and forefinger. "She had a coin."

This revelation led to another round of gasps.

"I am an adventurer currently in pursuit of the Lost City of Atlantis. I pieced together clues from ancient works of Grecian literature and art and found something of a code. When cracked, it led me to a set of coordinates, off the coast of Santorini. I believed the coin to be some kind of key. Only … I was expecting Atlantis. Not … well, wherever this is." She gave a small shrug, as though this were a mere point of interest, and not a colossal mistake.

We'd been sucked into a whirlpool and threatened to be turned into kibble for a giant sea serpent, and she could somehow brush it off with the ease of taking a wrong turn or missing a highway exit. It was equal parts impressive and infuriating.

"Is there at least a way for us to contact our loved ones?" I asked. "To let them know we're safe?"

Althea shook her head. "The wards that seal off the island tend to interfere with technology, including phone lines and internet signals. We don't have electricity. At least, not in the traditional way. Everything here is powered by magic."

"What do you do in case of an emergency?" Mom asked.

"We handle it," Althea replied, her tone forceful to the point of crispness. "My family has lived on this island for centuries. We know every inch. Every olive tree and cypress. Every creature that stirs in the cove. And my mother and her mother and all those before took care of themselves, and those who came here to seek shelter or aid. The goddesses of old look over us."

I licked my lips and resisted the urge to press for a better answer.

The woman at the head of the table frowned down at her tablet and tapped the screen a few times before shaking her head. "The internet is already down." Her frown deepened, revealing lines at either side of her mouth. After a few more fruitless taps, she set the tablet down on the table, the face of it pressed into the white and blue tablecloth. "So, they're just going to stay here?" the woman asked.

"It seems that way," Althea said. "Zora is making them a room now."

I frowned, wondering how she knew that, seeing as Trident had yet to return.

"This is Sophia," Althea continued, sweeping a hand toward the head of the table. "She is a member of the Sisterhood, but also lives here on the island full time, and works as my assistant."

Sophia stood up a bit straighter, shaking her glossy hair back. If I had to guess, I would have placed her in her early forties, with an athletic build and keen sense of style.

Althea continued the introductions, gesturing to the woman seated beside Sophia. "This is Ava," she said, then gestured to the opposite end of the table, "and her twin sister, Madeline."

The twins appeared to be somewhere in their early thirties, and while they shared identical features, there were stark differences in every other way, almost as though they tried to be the opposite of one another. Whereas Ava had dark hair, Madeline colored hers blonde. Madeline wore a floppy sun hat, adorned with flowers, and a white sundress. Ava wore a black tank top and jeans. Gold hoops adorned Madeline's ears and a gold bar necklace gleamed in the sun as she leaned back in her seat and sipped her water. Ava's only accessory was a pair of dark, oversized sunglasses that perched atop her head, along with her bun.

"This is Daphne," Althea continued, gesturing to a dark-skinned woman beside Madeline. "She is one of our two sisters from the underwater kingdom of Marindoria."

"You're a sea nymph?" I asked.

The woman nodded. Her dark hair was pulled to one side, fastened into a thick braid of many smaller braids. Pearls studded her earlobes, and two gold rings were stacked on each of the fingers of her right hand.

"There's Iris!" one of the other women announced, pointing out at the sea.

A figure emerged from the waves. As she stood from the gentle surf, her shimmering, fish-like tail melted away, revealing human legs. By the time she reached the beach, she was fully human in appearance, wrapped in a sea-green gown that clung to her damp skin.

Madeline got to her feet and waved with one hand while the other held her sunhat to her head, keeping it from blowing away in the breeze.

Althea beamed and gestured for the woman. "Iris!" she called out, beckoning enthusiastically. "Come, my dear. Hurry and join us."

The young woman—Iris—quickened her pace, ascending the steps to the deck with a grace I wouldn't have expected from someone who only occasionally used their legs. Heck, I used my legs every day and could still manage to stumble over my own feet.

Up close, I could see that her eyes were an other-worldly shade of blue-green like the deepest parts of the ocean, and combs of coral pinned back her long hair, which somehow was now dry. As well as her dress.

What in the world?

"I'm so sorry I'm late," Iris said, slightly out of breath. Her gaze swept over our group curiously. "I didn't realize we were expecting guests."

"We weren't," Trident muttered as he reappeared at Althea's side.

"Iris is our newest member," Althea explained to us, her tone warm with affection. "Now, let's see, remaining would be Lydia—" A woman with olive skin and a delicate heart-shaped face lifted a glass of wine in acknowledgement. "Thalia and Alexandra."

The last of the women nodded, though their expressions also remained guarded.

"You said you didn't mean to come here," Ava said. "And you explained how you found the door. But what made you think to drop the coin into the water? That seems … quite specific."

The question brought a smile to my aunt's face. There were few things she loved more than revealing the clever paths she took to find answers.

"There was a poem, in one of my research books, and I thought the cadence quite similar to one I had seen before, though that was in regard to souls beseeching Charon to take them on his riverboat. This one, however, was to the goddess Amphitrite and mentioned her sunken city. So, I thought, if a coin was needed to pay the ferryman, perhaps a coin might be needed to visit the Lost City."

Althea's thin brows lifted, but the rest of her face remained impassive as she asked her next question. "And the origin of the coin? They are quite rare."

"Ah." Aunt Lavender's smile widened. "Well, you don't spend more than half a century in the treasure hunting world and not wind up with a fistful of strings to pull. I had to trade my bronze-dipped phoenix feather and my entire collection of dragon scales. Not easy to come by, as I'm sure you can imagine!"

I looked at Selene and mouthed, "Dragon scales?"

She gave an irritated sniff. "It sounds more impressive than it was. She only had six."

Aunt Lavender twisted in her seat. "There were seven and you know it!"

"Six and a half, if I'm being generous."

"Might I ask for the name of the other party involved in such a trade?" Althea interjected.

Aunt Lavender's scowl twisted all the more as she righted herself in her chair. "Of course not!" she snapped. "That would go against treasure seeker code."

Althea's dark eyes flashed.

"Is Louka all right?" Daphne asked, concern in her dark eyes. "You didn't hurt him?"

Selene whipped her tail. "Oh, yes, as you can see, we came armed with bazookas and made him into a nice sushi dinner."

A round of gasps and angry muttering whizzed around the circle.

"Selene…" I growled.

"Louka is fine," Althea interjected, rising to her feet to refocus the room.

"Derelict of his duties, but fine," Trident added in a low grumble.

Daphne, the sea nymph, seethed, her arms folded over her chest. "How could you even joke about something like that?"

"It was a stupid question," Selene replied.

Trident's hackles rose.

"And I think it's time we get to ask some of the questions," Selene barreled onward. "For starters, what in Hades is this so-called *Sisterhood of Amphitrite*?" She dashed a pointed glance around the table as Iris went to sit beside Madeline. "Some sort of regressive sleepover for adults trying to relive their school days? Do you all wear matching silk pajamas and try to beat each other senseless with feather pillows?"

Another round of emphatic gasps and mutterings erupted from the gathered women, and it was all I could do to keep myself from sending my familiar into the sea on a cloud of air magic.

"I'm so sorry—" I began.

"I think that's enough questions for the time being,"

Althea said, elegantly sweeping to her feet once more. "Let's all take a breath. I need to check in with the kitchens and let Eleni know to set three extra plates for dinner."

"I think you mean *five*," Selene interrupted, her tail swishing ever more violently. "If you're planning on keeping us hostage, you'd better also plan on feeding us."

Althea's lips thinned but the corners curved into a tight smile. "Of course I would have Eleni set aside something for you and your more demure friend." She looked to Checkers, who sat obediently at my aunt's feet. He was, however, completely oblivious that he had become the center of attention, as his eyes followed a fly marching along the edge of the deck.

"Your room will be ready shortly. In the meantime, you can go anywhere on the island but stay out of the east wing for the time being. The final preparations for tonight's ceremony are still in progress."

I could feel vibrations of another half a dozen questions radiating from Selene, but before she could start shouting them out, I hauled her from the floor and clamped my arms around her as she thrashed and wriggled. "Unhand me! I'm a cat, Cora! Not a sack of potatoes!"

"I'll put you down once you stop struggling," I growled into her ear.

She jabbed her front paws into my chest and pushed, but I held fast.

"Trident will accompany you and ensure you don't get lost," Althea said, and while her tone was pleasant and a faint smile graced her face, the look in her eyes made it clear she was leaving no room for objection.

The black cat stared up at me, his yellow-green eyes intent and wary.

Right. Because I didn't have enough feline attitude in my life as it was.

With a heavy sigh, I turned and started toward the staircase off the deck, leading to the beach below.

At least our prison came with a nice view.

5

I stalked a good twenty yards in the sand before I plopped Selene down. "I'd ask what *that* was all about, but I know asking you to explain yourself would be in vain."

"You're acting like *I* was the rude one!" Selene replied, though she wasn't looking at me. Her focused scowl was fully locked onto our furry minder. "And you can tell your guardian I said so!"

Trident's tail fluffed up to twice its size, which, with his medium-length fur, was already quite full-bodied. "Don't make me get the serpent," he hissed.

"Tsk tsk. Such manners."

I rolled my eyes. "You're one to talk."

Selene flicked her glower toward me. "Whose side are you on here, Cora?"

"Mine!" I exclaimed, throwing my hands into the air. Then, looking at Mom and Aunt Lavender, I waved impatiently, willing one of them to step in and provide a little backup. "She can't really keep us here. Can she? Without any of our belongings?" I dug a hand into my pocket and fished out my phone. Predictably, it was waterlogged and the screen was black. "And no way to call home? Clint is going to be worried sick. He knows we were going out on the water today. When he doesn't hear from me, he'll assume the worst."

I bit back the beginnings of a panicked sob and stared out at the horizon, trying to calm my racing thoughts. The tranquil sea unfurled as far as the eye could see, its gentle rhythm a stark opposition to my pounding heart, without so much as the shadow or hint of another island, let alone a significant hunk of land.

"Calm down, Cora. Deep breaths," Mom said gently as she came to my side. She wrapped a comforting arm around my shoulders. "We'll figure this out."

"Quite right," Aunt Lavender chimed in. "Perhaps Selene can play nice with the sea serpent and see if he can deliver a message in a bottle for us."

Selene hissed in her general direction.

"Clint knew there was a chance we would lose contact. I told him so myself," Aunt Lavender added. "And he's not altogether unfamiliar with magical places. He saw the Fountain of Youth, after all."

Trident choked on a hairball. "Excuse me? What did you just say?"

Selene swung her glower across the sand. "Nothing that pertains to you, fuzzball."

"Your aunt is right," Mom said, still rubbing her thumb against my shoulder in soothing little circles. "Clint isn't the type to panic. And three days will go by before you know it. And we could have hardly asked for better accommodations. I mean, my goddess, this place is beautiful!" She drew in a deep breath and smiled before leaning closer and dropping her voice, "Imagine how much a place like this would cost per night!"

I couldn't help but smile along. Just a little.

Being trapped on a mysterious—and quite possibly enchanted—island wasn't exactly what I'd had in mind, but Mom deserved a vacation, and she was right. It was hard to complain when the sand was so warm and golden, and the sea so serene and blue.

"If you would like, I could show you around the house," Trident said. His tone was stiff, but the offer was kind.

"I wouldn't mind seeing about a litter box," Checkers said, looking around nervously. "All of this sand is making me a bit ... uh, eager."

Selene rolled her eyes. "Oh, for the love of— Checkers, have some decency!"

Aunt Lavender stifled a quiet laugh.

"Thank you, Trident," Mom said. "Lead the way."

The cat led us through a courtyard and back inside the house, but not to the main entry we'd already seen.

The hallways were wide and flooded with natural light, and even more art was displayed throughout.

"Aside from the living room, most of the common areas are in this wing," Trident explained, his tail swishing importantly as he padded across the polished marble floor. "The library is to your left, and straight ahead is the sitting room."

We followed him into an expansive room, painted with soft earth tones and creamy neutrals. Though it was hard to take much notice of the furnishings as a wall of windows stole the focus.

Aunt Lavender ran her hand over a particularly ornate side table. "These pieces must be hundreds of years old," she murmured, her eyes gleaming with interest.

Trident nodded. "Many of them have been in Althea's family for generations."

We continued through a series of rooms, each more impressive than the last. A music room housed a grand piano and various stringed instruments I couldn't name. A small conservatory was filled with exotic plants, their leaves glossy in the afternoon light.

As we climbed the stairs to the second floor, I took notice of the numerous portraits lining the wall.

"Those are past members of the Sisterhood," Trident explained. "Each has played a crucial role in our history."

The second floor was primarily guest rooms, all furnished in the same elegant, nautical-inspired style as the rest of the house. We'd returned to the first floor of the stately home when a middle-aged woman with silver-streaked hair bustled toward us from the opposite end of the hall.

"Ah, there you are, Zora," Trident said with a flourish of his tail. "Is the room ready?"

The woman paused, a twitch of irritation flickering across her face, though it was quickly suppressed as she offered a tight nod. "Yes. I'll bring towels as soon as I finish helping Eleni prepare for—"

"Supper," Trident cut in.

Zora frowned but nodded again. "Yes, supper."

"Excellent. Carry on." He flicked his tail in the other direction and the woman hurried on her way. "Zora is our housekeeper. She also lives on the island full time."

"Must be nice," I said a little under my breath. With the recent upswing in business at my candle shop and the winter tourist season barreling toward me, I could use a live-in housekeeper. Selene certainly wasn't picking up the slack.

We went back outside to survey the side gardens and another courtyard, this one with a burbling fountain. It was all breathtaking, but I couldn't keep my thoughts from veering back to Clint and envisioning him at home, calculating the time difference as he checked his phone and waited for me to call or text.

My worrying was interrupted by the sound of angry voices drifting from somewhere up ahead. Trident's ears perked and his pace slowed as he crept closer to the crack where a pair of glass doors were propped open to let in a breeze.

"You've had three months to take action on my suggestions," a woman said sharply. "And this is the best you can do? A box of crackers and some cheese? Unbelievable!"

I glanced through the windows and saw a large kitchen. As with the rest of the impressive estate, it looked like it had been copied from the pages of a high-end interior design magazine.

Two women squared off at the far end of the kitchen. A woman wearing a white chef's coat stood with her back to the windows, while one of the identical twins squared off, her hands balled at her hips. It was the blonde one. Madeline?

"You requested a gluten-free option for the charcuterie boards, which is why I purchased the herb crackers. They're made with almond flour. The additional varieties of cheese and fruit are also gluten-free," the chef said patiently. From her profile, I could see she had a peach-toned complexion and honey-blonde hair that was pulled back tightly and knotted at the nape of her neck.

"That was only one of half a dozen suggestions!" Madeline exclaimed, tossing her hands into the air. "It's always the same old thing. Don't you bore yourself? Is this what they're teaching in culinary schools? Oh, that's right. You didn't train professionally." She flashed an awful smile. "You're just some urchin Althea took

54

pity on and scooped from the sea. Well, here on land, we like a little flavor in our meals. See if you can't find some before dinner!"

With that, she spun on her stacked heels and stalked from the kitchen.

As soon as she'd gone, the chef's shoulders slumped forward, her head hanging for a moment.

A feline growl made me wince, but this time it wasn't Selene.

It was Trident.

"Excuse me," he said with clipped anger.

Without a sound, he slithered through the opening in the doors and went to speak with the chef in low tones.

"Come on," I said, beckoning for the others. "Let's give them some privacy."

Selene balked. "Privacy? If they want privacy, they can kindly let us off this island."

"Selene, you heard what Althea said. The magic doesn't work that way."

"Hmph." She plopped down on the hand-laid stone pathway. "Well, then I'll need some entertainment while I wait."

"Oh for Merlin's sake!" I shook my head and stalked off.

Mom leaned over to peek past me as I approached her and Aunt Lavender. "Is Selene coming?"

"She's too busy spying." I scoffed. "The only reason I agreed to come on this trip was to make her happy.

You'd think she could show her appreciation by, oh, I don't know, trying to not be a pain for a solid four hours. Is that really too much to ask?"

I glanced over my shoulder, shooting a pointed look at my familiar's back. She flicked her tail, as though sensing the heat of my glare.

Good.

"You didn't want to come on the trip?"

I blinked and snapped my head around to find my aunt peering at me with concern etched into the lines at the corners of her eyes.

"Oh—uh, well, it's not that I didn't want to—" I bit my lip. "I mean, it's beautiful, and everything, but..." I looked to Mom as I flailed for the right words.

Mom smiled, silently taking her cue. "You know Cora. She's a homebody."

I frowned. Okay, that wasn't quite how I would have put it.

"I didn't mean any offense, Aunt Lavender. I'm grateful you let me and the tiny demon tag along."

Checkers snickered. "Tiny demon."

"I'm glad to have you," Aunt Lavender said, lifting her chin to look over my shoulder. "And I suppose her, too. Though, I am waiting for her to launch into an 'I told you so' lecture any moment now."

I smiled. For all of Selene's faults—of which there were many—underneath her cranky exterior was a heart, and a fierce sense of loyalty to her guardians. She cloaked her concerns and worries in barbed words and sarcasm, but we all knew she cared in her own little hardheaded way.

At least, that's what I told myself to keep from throwing her into the lake on a weekly basis.

The demon cat in question trotted over, apparently having had her fill of gossip. Her tail was alert and eager, her expression pleased to the point of smugness.

"What?" I asked, my tone wary. "Why are you smiling?"

Selene looked up at me, her eyes sparkling. "Oh, nothing. I'm just rather impressed with Trident's colorful vocabulary. You know it tickles me when animals swear like drunken sailors."

My brow arched. "Selene, *you* swear like a drunken sailor."

"Exactly! And everyone knows how amusing I find it! What is your point?"

I rubbed my temples. "Maybe we should ask Trident to wrap up the tour and show us to our room. I think I need an aspirin and a nap before dinner."

As if summoned, our pint-sized host returned to us, his tail still quite fluffy in the aftermath of whatever had gone on in the kitchen. "Pardon the interruption," he said, swishing the fluffy plume in a wide arc, as though wishing to sweep the whole thing away. "I'll show you to your room. Dinner will be served promptly at seven o'clock, and there is to be a ceremonial blessing afterward. Althea will expect you to keep to your rooms and not wander during the ceremony. I'm sure you understand."

He cast a firm look at the five of us, ensuring there would be no argument.

To my surprise, Selene remained silent.

Satisfied, Trident turned with another swish of his tail and marched toward a pair of glass doors beyond those leading to the kitchen. He used a wisp of magic to open them and strutted through, his paws silent on the cool tiles.

6

*I*n the end, there wasn't enough time for a nap before dinner, but it was hard to complain when being put up in a free guest room with an unobstructed ocean view. Though, predictably, not all of us were dazzled by the accommodations. When I gasped and pointed out a dolphin in the distant waves, Selene told me I was letting Stockholm Syndrome win.

Aunt Lavender was too busy trying to unravel the secrets of the summoning magic to take much notice of the beauty surrounding us. "If I could just get that coin back, I'm sure I could figure it out," she muttered as we followed Trident down the hallway.

"It's a transportation spell," Selene replied, her tail lashing against my ankle.

"Will you stop that?" I slapped at the bare skin between my capri-length pants and my boat shoes. "It tickles. It's bad enough I'm covered in sand and salt."

"You don't suppose they'd let us use their washing machine, do you?" Mom asked.

Our clothes were dry, but our little dip in the Aegean clung to us all the same.

"I guess we can ask," I replied with a shrug. "Though, as nice as this place is, I didn't see fuzzy bathrobes in our room, so I'm not sure what we'd wear in the meantime."

Selene hit the end of her metaphorical tether and whipped around. "That's what you're worried about? Your *clothes*?!"

Trident appeared in the open doorway, a nonplussed look on his furry face. "Is everything all right?" he purred.

Selene flashed her teeth in his direction. "Mind your own business, puffball!"

Trident growled. "Keep it up, cat, and I'll see to it that Louka gets himself a little midnight snack. That is, if I could convince him to overlook your pungent scent."

I winced.

"Uh oh..." Checkers muttered, slinking behind Aunt Lavender's ankles to get clear of Selene's inevitable warpath.

Trident stalked into the room and the two cats circled one another like a pair of prize fighters waiting for the clang of the bell.

Selene shot a flurry of pink sparks over her head as her ears went flat. "It's clear you don't get out much, so let me be the first to break it to you—you're about as intimidating as a kitchen sponge, and you look like something some unfortunate soul had to dislodge from a shower drain!"

"Selene—" I warned.

"Keep talking," Trident replied. "It will only make it all the more satisfying when I hear you make a little *splash* into Louka's den."

Selene bared her teeth and hissed. "Well, then I hope you can swim, cause I'll be taking you with me!"

A flurry of pink sparks burst from Selene before I could rein back the magic. Fortunately, Trident was faster, and easily batted it away with a whip of his own borrowed magic.

Then he yawned. "Pathetic."

Selene sputtered and there was no doubt in my mind she was winding up for a second attempt, but Trident turned and padded back into the hallway. "Dinner will be getting cold," he called over his shoulder.

Selene growled and swore before swinging around, her glower once more fixated on us. "Did anyone see a tool shed on our little tour?"

"A tool shed?" I blinked. "What? Why?"

"I find myself in need of a chainsaw," Selene replied, her eyes aglow with menace. "Though a rusty pair of shrub clippers could work in a pinch."

I pinched the bridge of my nose. "All right, Rambo. That's quite enough."

We hurried to catch up with Trident and he led us back through the mansion to the deck off the main living room. It was nearing twilight, the sun having already bid the island goodnight, and someone had conjured glittering balls of light to float above the long table. The orbs bobbed in the salty breeze, casting magic light over an array of vibrant floral centerpieces, sparkling crystalware, and place settings ornamented in rich gold.

The chef, Eleni, and the housekeeper, Zora, worked to serve the table. Several bottles of wine were uncorked, and it was clear we were the last to arrive.

Althea sat at the head of the table, draped in a lilac-hued gown. A golden crown perched atop her head, with tines that looked like conical shells in between glittering rubies. She lifted her chin at our arrival, and the conversation and chatter ceased as she offered us a reserved smile. In the sudden—and awkward—silence, nearly a dozen pairs of eyes swiveled to cast curious glances in our direction.

"Ah, thank you for joining us," Althea said, gesturing to one end of the table, where three plates sat. Zora scurried over, a bottle of wine raised in silent question.

Mom nodded and offered a quiet "thank you" as she took the first seat.

"I trust the room is to your satisfaction?" Althea asked as we situated ourselves.

Trident stalked past Selene, whipping her in the

face with his tail as he hopped onto the seat at the far end of the table, opposite Althea.

I started to nod. "Oh, yes, they're—"

"Ahem!" Selene interrupted.

My nod turned to a flinch.

Althea's brows lifted. "Yes?"

"Are we supposed to eat on the floor like common mutts?"

"Where else would you eat?" Trident replied.

Chef Eleni turned to where a tray floated in midair and lifted a gold cloche to reveal three small crystal dishes, each filled with a heaping scoop of what looked like very expensive cat food. "I have roasted chicken, paired with a liver-infused gravy, and a side of braised sardines for texture."

Trident licked his whiskers and wiggled in his chair, his fluffy tail quivering slightly.

Apparently, the offer was so good that even Selene couldn't find fault. Undoubtedly, she also took some delight in receiving her meal before us mere humans.

Gradually, the chatter resumed as the women continued where they'd left off in their various threads of conversation. Iris, the sea nymph, was seated at Althea's right hand, and the older woman was listening intently as Iris spoke in hushed tones. From their expressions it seemed quite important, though I was too far away to catch so much as a snippet. Madeline and her twin sister were placed at opposite sides of the table once more, and it almost seemed as though they were making a deliberate effort not to look in one another's direction as they spoke with their respective neighbors.

Mom, Aunt Lavender, and I exchanged a look, but shrugged and made the most of it. I couldn't decide whether or not to be offended over being ignored. After all, we were not invited guests, and it was nice enough they had offered to share the meal with us. But at the same time, I couldn't help but wonder why Althea had bothered inviting us to the table if she had no plans to include us, or even to use it as an opportunity to pepper us with more questions about the events leading up to our unplanned arrival on her island.

The food was excellent. Everything was fresh and in season, and bursting with flavor. Selene and Checkers happily devoured their own meals, and as I glanced over at the post-dinner bathing, I cringed, knowing there was a zero percent chance Selene would just accept it as a one-time treat. As soon as we got home again, she'd be carrying on about liver-infused gravy and complaining that I never thought to offer her a proper side dish.

When I put down my fork and resisted the last bite of chocolate torte, a melodic chime like that of a harp sounded from somewhere inside the house, leading me to straighten in my seat. Before any of us could ask what the trill meant, all nine members of the Sisterhood set down their goblets and utensils and rose to their feet, in an almost Pavlovian response to the sound.

"Please, stay and finish your meal," Althea said. "Eleni and Zora will clean up when you're done. But when you are finished, I must insist you go straight to your rooms and remain there. It is imperative our ceremony not be interrupted."

This last part seemed aimed in Selene's direction, though she was too busy licking every bit of gravy from her whiskers to take notice.

I nodded my agreement and Mom joined me. "Understood."

Aunt Lavender hesitated but did not voice her objections.

"Good night," Althea said, then waved her hand and the other eight women trooped out in a single-file line, the twins taking their places at the very front and back of the procession.

Trident sat back in his seat and began cleaning his own face with graceful strokes of his fluffy paws. "And don't even think about trying anything," he said in between wiping down his whiskers. "Althea doesn't mess around when it comes to the ritual."

"Oh, yeah? And what's she going to do, kill us?" Selene scoffed.

Trident's eyes flashed. "It wouldn't be all that hard, you know. We still have your boat. There's nothing stopping her from sending it back through the ley line.

The coast guard would find it and assume it to be a terrible accident."

A chill went down my spine, both at the casualness of his tone and the realization that he was right.

FOR THE SAKE OF EVERYONE, we didn't linger at the table once our plates were cleared. Eleni offered more wine, or perhaps an espresso, but we declined and followed Trident back across the estate to our assigned room.

As soon as the door closed, a soft *pop* signaled the door was locked and, likely, warded from the outside, and a muffled Trident bid us good evening.

"Well, looks like we won't be getting any room service," I muttered. Not that I had room for another bite.

"Oh, look!" Mom exclaimed.

I turned and found her pointing at the foot of the bed where three nightgowns and pairs of satin slippers were laid out.

"How cute, you can all match when you get ceremonially murdered and thrown into the sea." With a scoff, Selene stalked across the room and vaulted onto the nearest windowsill.

I shot her a dark look. "Enough, Selene. No one is getting murdered."

"The whole thing is a little weird, though," Mom said, her voice quiet. "That strange chime and the way they all got up in unison, like robots." She shivered.

I nodded and gathered up one of the nightgowns. "Agreed."

"What do you know about Amphitrite?" Aunt Lavender asked, directing the question to Selene's back.

The curtains were pulled back, revealing the shimmers of the full moon reflecting off the waves, and Selene stared at the water. "It's all a bunch of superstition if you ask me. It's not as if the gods need mortals for anything beyond an ego pat or petty amusement."

"I don't know, Selene. It's not like the days of old," Aunt Lavender said. "Time has changed things. You know that better than most."

This remark rankled the cat, and her fur bunched around the base of her neck. "You don't need to remind me. *Time* is the one thing I don't want to talk about."

Mom and I shared a look.

"All right. I'm taking a shower," I announced. "I'll be quick, I promise."

Mom smiled. "Go right ahead, dear."

There didn't appear to be a clock in the room, and with all of our phones damaged, it was hard to know how much time passed. But when we'd all showered and changed into our borrowed nightgowns—despite Selene's heckling—I imagined it had to be getting close to midnight. Or, at the very least, my eyes felt like it must be.

The door to the room was locked, but Selene managed to get the window open a bit to let in some of the cool night air. The sound of the ocean was calming, and as I lay down on the bed nearest the windows, I tried to focus my mind on the soft roar of the sea and not on the image of Clint sitting at home, his phone in one hand, the other resting on Pippin's worried head.

"People are coming back up the beach," Selene hissed after a few minutes. She was still positioned in the window, like a stony gargoyle, keeping watch.

"Are you going to the springs, Daphne?" one of the women asked. I couldn't tell who the voice belonged to.

A soft snore sounded from the other side of the bed, and I glanced over to see Mom, her hands resting on her stomach.

Aunt Lavender and Checkers were still awake, though, and crept toward the window. I frowned but managed to push myself upright and followed suit.

"I saved some of my dinner for Louka," Daphne replied, with a flash of a smile, her white teeth all the more striking in the dark.

"Well, it certainly wasn't fit for humans," another voice said.

Sure enough, it was Madeline.

"Yeesh, she's really got a bone to pick with that chef, huh?" Aunt Lavender said quietly.

"You don't have to be so rude, you know," another voice interjected.

To my surprise, it belonged to Ava. Madeline's twin. It was the first time I'd seen them interact.

"No one asked you," Madeline snapped, her arms folding across her chest.

From the looks of it, they'd all changed into matching robes, the material shiny in the moonlight. I glanced down at my own borrowed night clothes. Was there just a closet somewhere, stuffed full of silk robes and pajamas? And if so, why?

"Come on," another voice said. "It's late. We're all tired."

I pressed closer to the window and saw Iris stepping between the two sisters. She smiled sweetly and took Madeline by the arm. "Come on," she said, giving it a gentle tug. "You still need to tell me about this new beau of yours!"

Ava barked a dry laugh. "I think the term you're looking for is sugar daddy."

"Ava, why don't you just—"

Iris gave a harsher tug and managed to pull Madeline away.

Daphne and Ava watched them go, then turned and departed, striding up the beach a ways until they were out of our line of sight.

"You know, maybe you weren't too far off with your comparing this thing to a high school slumber party," I told Selene. "Seems like some of them have really nailed the whole mean girls vibe."

I trudged back to the bed, my limbs feeling every bit as heavy as my eyelids. Selene stayed in the window a bit longer, but eventually, I felt her jump up onto the foot of the bed.

Sleep didn't come as easily as I expected, though, and I found myself tossing and turning as much as I could manage without disturbing Mom. With a grunt, I fluffed up the feather pillow and nestled down again, my mind churning.

"Cora..." Selene said quietly.

"I know." I sighed. "Sorry. I just hate that I can't call Clint."

There was silence for a moment, then the subtle weight of a tail coming to rest on my legs. "It will be all right, Cora. Try and get some sleep."

I reached into the darkness and stroked down Selene's side. Only once. And she didn't protest.

At some point I slipped into a deep sleep, only to be awoken by a blood-curdling scream.

7

*E*arly morning light flooded the room, leaving me disoriented as I jolted upright in bed. "What was that?"

Aunt Lavender was already scrambling out of bed. With relief, I saw Mom lurch through the bathroom door, a hand towel clasped to her chest and a glob of toothpaste on her cheek. "Cora?!" she exclaimed, sagging with visible relief when she saw me.

"I'm fine." I got to my feet, my heart pounding in my ears. "Where did that come from, though?"

"Somewhere down the hall, I think." Aunt Lavender went to the door and tried the doorknob. "It's still locked!" she growled.

The screaming stopped as abruptly as it had begun, which in some ways only added to the ominous uncertainty.

"This is ridiculous. We should've never let them

trap us in here, like dogs in a cage," Selene grumbled. She paced the length of the room, her tail twitching violently with each step.

She stopped at the far end of the room, her hindquarters backed up all the way to the sliver of wall beneath the long windows. "All right. Step aside!" she exclaimed, her blue eyes blazing with intense concentration as she lowered her head and raked her paws on the thin rug, looking like a bull about to charge a matador.

I swung my legs over the side of the bed. "Selene..."

She charged, sending a flurry of pink sparks whipping into a frenzy as she bounded across the room. At the last second, she flung the magic ahead of her like a cannonball and leaped.

Before the magic hit the door, it opened, and both Selene and the torrent of magic barreled into Trident.

I swore loudly as the two cats and the ball of magic hit the other side of the hallway with a loud *thump* that quickly exploded into hissing and yowling and the sound of pottery breaking.

"Selene!" I ran to the doorway, careful to swerve around Checkers as he peeked into the hallway. "Everyone okay?" he asked in his quiet voice.

Aunt Lavender made a grab for Checkers before he could get involved.

Trident spoke quickly in Greek, and while I didn't have a handle on even the basics of the language, it was quite obvious that none of the words were meant to be nice or polite. The black cat's hackles were still on end, giving him the look of a proper Halloween cat, while Selene lay stunned on her side, having hit the wall first. Shards of pottery lay scattered between them, and a sizable dent marred the wall behind the place the painted vase once stood on display.

I didn't even want to think about how much that was going to cost me to replace.

Selene hunkered low, ready to pounce, and offered a few of her own retorts in Trident's native language.

"No!" I said, whipping up a barrier of wind magic and dividing the hallway between the two felines. The field was invisible, but strong enough to ruffle the fur of both cats. "No one is going to kill anyone. It was a mistake, Trident. We heard someone screaming, and we were trying to get out of our room, that's all."

The black cat glared at Selene through the invisible shield, unrelenting.

Aunt Lavender stomped her foot. "Enough of this. Tell us what's going on. Who was screaming, and why?"

At that, Trident turned his head, his chartreuse eyes dancing with malice and magic. He shot a final glower at Selene before straightening, his fur beginning to smooth back down against his lean body.

"Let me at him! Let me at him!" Selene taunted.

"Not on your ninth life, cat!"

"There isn't time for this," Trident snapped. "Althea needs to see you."

"Which one of us?" Mom asked.

Trident cast a look around, his expression souring slightly before he replied, "All of you. There's been something of an incident, and if one of you has healing magic, you'd best come with me."

I dropped the wind magic partition, keeping my eyes on Selene to ensure she didn't attempt a feline version of a sucker punch.

Fortunately, Trident had said something that interested her enough to temporarily abate her thirst for vengeance. "Incident?" she repeated. "What kind of incident?"

Trident glowered at her but continued. "Have you heard of Charybdis lace?"

"Of course. What do I look like, some kind of remedial apprentice?" Selene puffed out her chest.

I looked to Mom, then Aunt Lavender. Both of them shrugged.

Apparently, we were remedial apprentices by Selene's metric. Good to know.

"It's nasty stuff," Selene continued. "Don't tell me you keep some of it around the island. It's highly invasive."

Trident heaved a heavy sigh. "Brilliant analysis," he muttered with heavy sarcasm. "Unfortunately, the serpent likes it, and therefore, Althea keeps it around. Besides, the stuff is nearly impossible to eradicate—at least not without using toxic products that could disrupt other ecosystems here on the island."

"All that screaming was for a rash? Who fell into the

itchy patch?" Selene asked, a little too jauntily, all things considered.

"No one fell into the lace. They were poisoned with it."

Selene reared back. "Poisoned? You're saying someone ingested it?" She shook her head. "I don't know what you expect us to do about it. That's dead-witch-walking territory. How did something like that even accidentally end up in someone's food?"

Trident waited a beat.

Selene nodded. "Ah. We have a murderer on the island. Great. Just when I thought this little staycation of ours couldn't get any better."

She flicked her tail and marched closer to Trident. His tail went rigid, but he didn't back down.

Selene flashed her teeth. "Lead the way."

TRIDENT LED us down the rear staircase and to a small room not far from the kitchen, if I was properly oriented. The room's layout was something akin to a medical clinic, with a sterile-looking bed, draped in a white cloth, and a bank of small beige cabinets hung over a small counter and washing station.

Althea had her back to us as she stood hunched over the woman on the bed. She turned at our footsteps and I realized it was Madeline who lay there, wearing a nightgown identical to the ones we wore, leading me to once again wonder about the seemingly enforced dress code. Or were all the matching outfits just meant as a convenience for the Sisterhood's quarterly meetings?

Madeline's sun-kissed skin looked pale now, but for the red welts along her arms, neck, and face. They looked like hives or the beginnings of a nasty rash, ranging in size from that of a dime to a half dollar. Her lips were swollen and red, and aside from the rise and fall of her chest, she didn't seem to be moving.

Althea looked to her familiar, an unspoken question in her steely eyes.

"The loudmouth cat knows what Charybdis lace is."

The lines around Althea's lips tensed as she nodded in Selene's direction. "You have experience with it?"

Selene marched past Trident, brushing against him slightly, body-checking him as she went. Trident growled.

"You're sure it's Charybdis lace?" she asked as she approached the unconscious woman.

"Look at the marks. Perfect concentric circles, like—"

"Tentacle marks."

"Her temperature is spiking. She's been unresponsive since we found her. Breathing is shallow and too fast. I don't have an antidote."

"And you're sure she ate it?"

A pained expression gripped Althea's face as she checked the woman's vitals. For a remote island, the small clinic seemed quite well equipped. An electronic monitor kept track of the vitals, the same as would be found in any modern hospital. A tank of oxygen stood in one corner, ready for use.

"Traces of it were found in a bowl of soup on the nightstand in her room."

Selene scoffed. "That's one heck of a way to garnish a soup."

Althea's lips pressed into an even thinner line.

"So, you suspect poisoning, then?"

"I don't want to make any assumptions—"

"And I don't want to be stuck on this island with a killer running around! We don't always get what we want, do we?"

"Selene," I said softly.

Althea raised a hand, dismissing my concern. "No, she's right. It's just … unthinkable."

"Where did the soup come from? Has anyone searched the kitchen?" Selene asked.

Althea's shoulders slumped as her gaze fell to the unconscious woman. She brushed her thumb over the back of the woman's hand, careful not to disturb the IV line. "I don't know. Are you sure there's nothing we can do? No antidote? If it was topical, I have a salve that could help, but something like this…" Her words trailed off, her eyes squeezing shut.

Selene looked up. "Where's the one with the fins?"

"Fins?"

"The nymph. She can get a message out, can't she? We're stuck here, but can the fish and sea life come and go? We need them to find a specific type of kelp. It can be made into a paste."

"What is it called? Is it native to the Aegean?"

Selene nodded. "I can't recall the name, but I know what it looks like. The sea nymphs will know it."

Althea blinked, then rose to her full height once more, determination settling in to banish the lines from her face, at least temporarily. She looked to Trident, and an unspoken communication passed between them. The black cat hurried from the room with clipped, purposeful strides.

"You're doing what you can," Selene said, in an almost uncharacteristically charitable tone. "In the meantime, we can help track down who did this. But you have to let us have access to the full island, and no more of this locking us up at night business. Got it?"

Althea hesitated, but only for a moment. She nodded her agreement. "Yes, of course. I'll be sure to let the others know."

Selene flicked her tail as she turned to the door. She glanced up at us, still stunned, on her way past. "Come on, ladies. Looks like we have some investigating to do."

I exhaled slowly through parted lips, giving Mom and Aunt Lavender a wary look as we fell into step behind the cat. I paused at the doorway to glance back over my shoulder, where Althea was leaning over Madeline's body, whispering something. A single tear fell down the woman's cheek and splashed onto the white sheet.

My heart squeezed, and I hurried to catch up to the others.

8

"*N*ow we have to solve an attempted murder? Why do bad things always happen to good cats?" Selene muttered as we continued down the hallway.

I frowned at her. "You say that like you're not the one who just volunteered us for the job!"

"And like you're a good cat," Aunt Lavender added.

"Well, that, too," I agreed. Then, after a quick glance over my shoulder, added, "We shouldn't be getting involved in this, Selene."

"No? So, then what's your plan? Go back to our room and let them lock us up and hope we don't go mad? Hard pass!"

"You're being impossible!" I looked at Mom. "She's being impossible."

"That may be, but she's not entirely off base," Aunt Lavender said.

Selene swished her tail, as though chalking up an invisible point for herself. "Thank you, Lavender."

"It's clear something is going on, and if we can do some good, it seems like the right thing to do."

Selene's pacing slowed as she swiveled a slow glance over her shoulder, casting a decidedly suspicious look in my aunt's direction. "Wait a second. This isn't about helping. You're thinking if we help them with their little problem, they'll tell us what they know about Atlantis."

Aunt Lavender's lips twitched, but she neither confirmed nor denied Selene's accusation.

Beside me, Mom groaned.

I shook my head. "So what do you expect us to do? Run around this whole island, playing Matlock in our slippers and nightgowns? Very professional."

Trident appeared at the opposite end of the hall, coming toward us with his usual aloof posture. Selene swore darkly, her fur standing on end.

I bumped her hindquarters with the toe of my slipper. "Easy."

Behind him, Zora, the housekeeper, bustled along with a stack of neatly folded laundry in a wicker basket.

"If you're here to tell us to go back to our prison, too late," Selene said with an air of triumph.

Trident flicked his tail. "Althea already told me. Hence why I found Zora and had her bring your clothing to you. Unless you'd rather your companions

81

go parading about like that." He gave us two-leggeds a scathing look.

Selene found this amusing and snickered under her breath. Apparently, the two cats could find some common ground—so long as it came at our expense.

Charming.

Trident continued, "Though, I'll state for the record I think it's a bad idea to let you get involved in this matter."

This amused Selene even further. She all but beamed at him.

"Here you are," Zora said, stepping between the two cats to offer me the basket. "If you need anything else, please let me know. It's unbelievable what's happened."

"Thank you for this," I said as I settled the basket against my hip.

Zora twisted her hands together, the backs of which were dotted with age spots. "Daphne and Iris went to speak with the fish," she added softly.

I did my best to pretend that was a normal sentence.

"No one can come or go during the ritual, but the fish can relay messages. You really think there's a cure?"

"I wouldn't say cure," Selene replied, her tone earnest for once. "But it will help give her a chance."

Zora chewed the corner of her thin lips, then jolted from her thoughts and gave a quick nod. "I need to get back to the kitchen to help Eleni with breakfast."

We repeated our appreciation for the laundered clothing and she departed, scurrying with quick steps until she vanished around the corner. I vaguely wondered if she'd come across the broken vase yet, and winced.

Selene looked to Trident. "Just to confirm my suspicion, it was Madeline we saw in the kitchen yesterday afternoon, right? The one berating the chef?"

Trident stared at her, unblinking. "What are you saying?"

Selene tilted her head in an "oh, come on" expression.

Trident's eyes narrowed. "That was, indeed, Madeline. Though, I take issue with your rush to judgment."

"Take issue all you want. No fur off my tail." Selene sniffed.

Trident bristled. "Eleni has worked for Althea for the better part of a decade. The two of them are as close as sisters. Eleni understands how important the Sisterhood is, both to Althea and—" He stopped short. "Eleni is a professional. She would never stoop to poisoning someone over complaints about her food."

"Why is everyone so cagey about this whole secret ritual thing? What are you people really up to?"

Trident swished his tail, sweeping away the question. "That's none of your concern. You may have wheedled your way into this unfortunate situation, but you have no right to ask questions about the Sisterhood."

I frowned. "It seems it could be relevant though, wouldn't you say?"

Trident shifted his narrowed gaze in my direction. "Which is precisely why I told Althea you shouldn't get involved. But—" He stopped and went rigid, the tips of his ears quivering slightly as his eyes took on a faraway look. The moment passed in the blink of an eye, and his expression returned to its usual mix of ire and irritation. "Everyone is gathering on the deck. I suggest you get changed and meet us out there. Undoubtedly, you'll have questions to ask."

"I want to see the scene—I want to see Madeline's room first," Selene argued. "Where the soup was found."

"And I want a sunfish the size of a Christmas ham delivered to my bedside table every morning. But some things just aren't going to happen."

With that, he stalked off.

"Sunfish? Blech. Far too bony. But then, I suppose it's only natural he'd have bad taste. He's too sheltered. It's obvious he wasn't properly socialized as a kitten."

I pinched the bridge of my nose, my eyes sliding closed. "Selene, would it be so much to ask that you *not* antagonize our host further?"

"Obviously, Cora." Selene sniffed. "Besides, I'm only giving him what he's putting out there. When he starts behaving better, I'll think about reining in my disdain."

I shook my head. Mom patted my arm.

"What was that whole thing there in the middle? Did you see the way he froze up?" Aunt Lavender asked, gesturing with one finger in a circular motion where the cat had stood moments ago.

"I don't know. Maybe he lost his train of thought?"

Aunt Lavender pursed her lips but offered no theory of her own.

Mom took the laundry basket from me. "Come, let's go get changed. I think we'll feel better when we're in clean clothes again."

Aunt Lavender followed after her. "I don't know. These satin slippers are quite nice. Do you think they'd let me take them home?"

My fingertips raked through my short, cropped waves and I found a stray feather from my pillow tangled in the mess. At least Selene hadn't noticed I was molting. I'd never hear the end of it.

WE DRESSED QUICKLY and made our way back through the house to the deck where we originally met the members of the Sisterhood. The sun was warm, but not overbearing, especially in the shade from the pergola, where a gentle breeze stirred the overhanging vines.

Eleni bustled around the table and spoke in low

tones as she offered to refill coffee cups and glasses of fresh juice. Two trays of delicate pastries sat at either end of the table, with several smaller platters laid out in between, bearing several types of fruit, breakfast meats, and a gourmet quiche topped with fresh herbs. It appeared the chef was either one of those "the show must go on" types, or perhaps she used her work as a way to distract herself, as exquisite care had been taken to oversee every detail of the meal. The strawberries had been sliced and fanned out, with a single grape placed in the center, to make them appear like blossoms nestled among segments of dark blood orange and persimmons. The pastries looked homemade, meaning she must have been up for hours.

I tried to catch the woman's eye as she made her way around the table, but she kept her chin tucked, going about her duties with the efficiency and precision of a trained professional whose goal was to not draw attention to herself as she worked.

Zora hadn't rejoined the group, but a quick headcount revealed everyone else was there. Even Madeline's twin sister, Ava, which struck me as a bit odd. She sat at the head of the table, where Althea had sat the night before, delicately picking at a slice of spinach quiche in between sips of coffee.

There had been some tension between the two women on the beach the night before, but it struck me as odd not only to find her absent from her sister's bedside but also to see her acting so casual. I reminded myself not to judge, though. Not everyone handles a crisis in the same way. Perhaps her detached mannerisms were the only thing keeping her from breaking down.

A few of the women looked up at our arrival and Selene wasted no time taking the spotlight. She jumped onto a chair, placed her front paws on the edge of the table, and panned an appraising look down the breakfast spread, her whiskers quivering slightly. "No fish, huh?" She shot an accusatory glance toward Trident, as though this were some personal failing on his part.

Trident, for his part, narrowed his eyes and twitched his tail. But before he could tell her off for her rudeness, Chef Eleni cleared her throat. "Fish? I have some smoked salmon. Would that be of interest? It was meant to be for this afternoon, but I'm sure there's no harm in bringing it out now."

Selene flashed her teeth in a triumphant smile. "I think that would do quite nicely. Let me help you with that."

Her feline grin only widened as Trident realized what she was up to.

Selene jumped down with a dainty hop and followed quickly on the chef's heels. I exchanged a look with Mom and Aunt Lavender, and took my leave, knowing Selene couldn't be left to her own devices. At least, not wholly without supervision. As we returned inside, I heard Aunt Lavender exclaiming about the color of the oranges before asking if someone could pass the quiche.

"Terrible mess, this business with the Charybdis lace, isn't it?" Selene asked the chef as we followed her to the kitchen.

Eleni faltered a bit but quickly covered the misstep and continued forward. "Yes. Nothing like this has ever happened before."

"That seems hard to believe."

I scowled, though Selene didn't even appear to notice.

"It does?" Eleni asked, glancing over her shoulder. The look of confusion on her face seemed earnest to me.

"I think Selene just means—"

"I'll be speaking for myself, thank you very much," Selene snapped.

Eleni's brows lifted as she looked at me.

"You get a gaggle of women here, all from different walks of life, and trap them on an island for three days every quarter? Come on. There has to be some drama. Friendships. Rivalries. After all, it's not like Althea keeps her favoritism closely guarded. I've been here less than twenty-four hours and can see fault lines left, right, and center."

Eleni bristled, her steps becoming even more clipped. "I'm sure I don't know what you mean."

"Why isn't Ava at her sister's bedside?" Selene

pressed, her own pace quickening to close the gap. "Why were they arguing on the beach last night after this so-called *ritual?* Which, I also have half a dozen questions about, when we have the time."

We reached the kitchen and Eleni hurried ahead, making a beeline for the sink. "I can't tell you about the ritual. I'm not a member of the Sisterhood, and have never attended the ritual itself." She grabbed a sponge and began furiously scrubbing at the spotless-looking counter.

"Look, the way I see it, the Charybdis lace was in Madeline's soup. Soup that I have to assume came from this kitchen." Selene slowly stalked around the island. "*Your* kitchen."

Eleni's hand stilled as the implication of Selene's words sank in, and she snapped upright.

"I didn't serve her the soup! I didn't even make the soup. It came from a can!" She shuddered as though the very idea caused physical pain. "Althea insists we keep some in the pantry, along with the dry goods, in case of emergency. I always tell her that even in a disaster I could manage to make a proper soup, but she buys the cans anyway. Ugh!"

Selene crouched. "Seems all the more reason to use the canned soup then. Muddy up the trail. Cover your tracks."

Eleni's eyes turned beseeching as she looked to me for help. "Please, you can't listen to her. I didn't do anything. Why would I poison Madeline?"

I grimaced. "We, uh, sort of overheard you and her yesterday afternoon. It sounded pretty heated."

Eleni reared back as though I'd slapped her across the face. "What?" Recognition dawned before I could elaborate and she exhaled a strained laugh. "Oh, I see. Because she complained about my food? You think I tried to hurt her over that?!"

"Maybe you wanted to silence her complaints once and for all," Selene replied in her best impersonation of a prime-time detective with a hot lead.

Eleni scoffed and shook her head as she resumed her scrubbing. "That was nothing new. Ever since her divorce, Madeline's been prickly about everything. The bedding isn't soft enough. The pillows are too fluffy, or not fluffy enough. The slippers are too tight. The shower grout is dull. The lettuce is too wilted, the meat too salty, the cake not sweet enough. On and on it goes. She drives me and Zora to drink."

"Does Althea know about all of this?" I asked. She didn't strike me as the type of woman who would put up with such things. And Trident certainly hadn't seemed happy when we'd overheard Madeline dressing Eleni down in the kitchen.

"Oh, most of it," the chef replied. "There's not much that happens on the island that she doesn't know about. But the Sisterhood is a lifetime appointment. So, we all grin and bear it, and thank Amphitrite this only has to happen once a quarter."

"And why is that?" Selene asked, her tone no longer

sharp and demanding, and more of a soft, inquisitive purr.

Eleni skewered her with a look. "Madeline gets under my skin. I won't lie. But I didn't serve her the soup and I certainly didn't try to poison her. As soon as I finished cleaning up after dinner, I closed the kitchen down and went to my cottage, it's just up the hill."

"Did anyone see you headed that way?" I asked.

Eleni rinsed out the sponge and placed it back in the shallow dish beside the sink. She heaved a sigh as she turned back to face us. "I said goodnight to Zora when we passed in the hall, but everyone else was busy with the ritual. You'll have to take my word for it." She paused and folded her arms. "Why are you even asking about all of this? Does Althea know you're going around interrogating her staff?"

"She asked for their help," a voice said from behind us. Turning, we found Trident padding into the room. "They were magically sealed into their quarters all night, so technically speaking, they are the only ones we can say for sure had nothing to do with what's happened to Madeline."

Eleni's expression softened in the presence of the cat. "How is she?"

"Althea is doing her best to keep her stabilized. Daphne and Iris sent word with the fish to see if someone from their kingdom can help." Trident looked over at Selene, then lifted his gaze to meet my own. "I think that's enough questions for now. Althea has given me permission to take you to Madeline's room."

Selene perked. "Finally."

We followed Trident as he turned back around, but I took note of the sag of relief in Eleni's shoulders as the cat ushered us from the kitchen.

9

"*N*eed I remind you we are on a very small island, with a very small number of people, most of whom already seem a bit on the hostile side. So, could you maybe holster the double-barrel barrage next time?"

Selene stalked ahead of me, not so much as missing a single stride at my scathing words. "If they already hate us, I don't see what harm we can do."

She swished her tail.

"Oh, I don't know, maybe push us out to sea to play with their guard dog."

"Meh. I could take him."

"Okay, Cujo." I rolled my eyes. It truly was a wonder that after all this time the cat could still manage to catch me off guard with her bravado.

"Fine," I huffed. "Suit yourself. I'll stock up on popcorn and sell tickets for ringside seats."

I veered past her and stormed down the hall. In truth, my two legs were no match for her four, but she let me have my moment and I reached the outdoor deck ahead of her. Aunt Lavender sat at the table, inspecting a slice of strawberry she'd skewered with the tines of her gold-plated fork. "These might be the best tasting strawberries I've ever had. Where do they come from?" She paused, then glanced over the rest of the spread. "Where does any of this come from?"

"Really, Lavender, that's what you're worried about right now?" Selene asked from behind me.

Aunt Lavender offered a half-hearted shrug before popping the piece of fruit into her mouth.

"We're somewhat familiar with hidden communities," Mom began to explain, glancing around at some of the members who lingered over their own breakfasts. "We live in a town called Winterspell. It's in Washington State. You might have heard of it?"

She smiled, but no one so much as acknowledged the question.

Mom's lips thinned slightly as she lifted the linen napkin from her lap and dabbed the corners of her mouth. "Well, in any case, it's a small town. Or at least it used to be—it definitely feels like it's bordering on a big town these days. But it's magic residents only. The Arcane Order put in protective wards to conceal the whole thing from sight. As the town grows, it does get a little harder to bring goods in and out without attracting attention. Of course, the Arcane Order has agents strategically placed within non-magical law enforcement, but still, it never hurts to be cautious. And sometimes it gets hard relying on—"

One of the women—Alexandra, I thought—offered Mom a polite smile. "It sounds like a nice place to live. Most of us live in the magical world, too. In and around Greece."

"And every quarter, you travel through some sort of portal to get here?" I asked, taking the empty chair beside Mom.

Trident cleared his throat, a silent reminder that we were meant to be elsewhere. I stood again. "Right. We were going to go take a look at Madeline's room—"

That got Ava's attention. Her head snapped up, and she set her coffee cup on the table a little too roughly, sending some of its contents splashing down the side. She let out a hiss as the hot liquid met her fingers. "What do you mean, 'look in Madeline's room'?" she snapped, quickly brushing her hand with her napkin. "What right do you have to go rummaging through her things?"

"We're trying to figure out what happened to her," I began.

"So what, now you're detectives or something?" Ava fired back. She peeled her napkin from her hand and looked down at the red splotch where the hot coffee had singed her, her scowl deepening. "This whole thing is ridiculous. You shouldn't even be here, and now you're sticking your noses where they don't belong."

Some of the others looked between us, torn between taking Ava's side and not wanting to draw her ire.

"We're just trying to help," I said, keeping my tone steady.

"And, since you asked, we have quite a bit of experience with this," Selene interjected. "Winterspell is a fine place to live, but you wouldn't believe the stories we could tell about the old buffoon that used to run our town's police department. Let's just say, he left a lot to be desired in the sheriffing department. And so, when we needed to, we stepped up. Which is what we're doing now. It seems that you, of all people, should welcome our help in figuring out what happened to your sister."

Ava glowered at Selene. "I don't think I like your tone, cat."

Selene flashed her teeth. "And I don't think I care."

Ava stared darkly at each of us in turn, then threw her napkin onto the table and pushed her chair back so hard, it nearly toppled over as she stormed back inside the house.

Selene looked around, as though daring anyone else to raise their objections. Suddenly, everyone became very interested in the bits of quiche and fruit left on their plates.

Selene flashed a victorious grin, then hopped off her chair and stalked over to where Trident stood. "I suppose we're still stuck with you as our tour guide?"

"Trust me, the only tour I want to take you on is of the deep-sea variety," Trident replied, twitching his tail and walking away.

I caught Mom's eye, and a look of acknowledgment passed between us. With a smile, she reached for the serving fork in the quiche and politely asked if anyone would mind if she took the last slice.

Aunt Lavender followed me, but she waited until we were out of earshot of the table before leaning in. "If anyone can get them to talk, it'll be Lilac."

I smiled and gave a nod. "My thoughts exactly."

Aunt Lavender smiled back.

We followed Trident to the second floor, where the hallway to the guest rooms branched off to the left and right. A marble bust of a woman stood guard at the end of the hall, with flowing locks so detailed and fluid-looking it was hard to believe they were carved from stone. All of the art in the house was stunning and had a look that suggested it had been gathered over decades, perhaps even centuries. As we continued down the hall, I couldn't take my eyes off a seascape painting in a gold-plated frame with tiny carvings depicting various sea creatures.

"How long has Althea been here on the island?" Aunt Lavender asked Trident.

"The Zosimos family has protected this island for over seven hundred years. It's something of a long story, and not mine to tell. All you need to know is that the goddess Amphitrite herself entrusted this estate to them, and it will remain that way, so long as the goddess wills."

"Why is everything so secretive?" Checkers asked, making his little voice heard for the first time that morning. Checkers was a far simpler creature than Selene, having only been part of the magic world for a little over two years. He was a dutiful familiar and a wonderful companion to my aunt, but he had a more simplistic view of the world, lacking the many decades of experience that gave Selene her sharp insights.

I, for one, appreciated his almost childlike wonder and fascination with all things human and magic. He was a refreshing change of pace, especially when stacked up against Selene's jaded cynicism.

Trident looked over his shoulder, his furry face pinched, as though unsure what to make of the adolescent cat. "The Sisterhood has a sacred duty to uphold. No one outside the Sisterhood is supposed to even know this place exists. Disruptions, such as your presence here, could be cataclysmic. You're a familiar, aren't you? Surely you must have some knowledge of the delicate balance of the world. Some things can't be disrupted without dire repercussions."

Checkers gave a sage nod, but he still looked a little bewildered.

"Checkers is only newly part of the magic world," Selene rushed to interject. "Thanks to me, of course. You're welcome, by the way," she added as an aside to the black-and-white cat. "You see, I used to be this one's familiar—" She gestured toward my aunt with the tip of her tail, "—and now I am *this* one's familiar." She flicked her tail toward me.

Trident stopped walking and turned fully around to face us. "But she's still alive?" he said, looking at Aunt Lavender as though suddenly uncertain of this fact.

Aunt Lavender laughed good-naturedly. "An astute observation," she said with a chuckle.

"It's a very long story, involving kidnappers, and cursed candles, and a backstabbing treasure hunter being turned to stone—" She stopped and blinked. "Although, all things considered, I suppose you are pretty familiar with the whole people turning to stone thing."

I hadn't yet seen a piece of art featuring a gorgon or Medusa herself, but it wouldn't surprise me to find one somewhere on the estate.

"I see," Trident said, though the slow, drawling cadence of the words suggested otherwise.

"We used a familiar bonding spell," I explained. "It severed the tether between Selene and my aunt, and bonded her to me."

Trident frowned. "I've heard of the familiar bond, but only in the context of an animal bonding to its first guardian, not simply because they've chosen another." He lifted his chin, and the long fur on his chest ruffled out. "Of course, I would never consider such a thing. It's a matter of duty!"

Selene growled. "I *said* it was a long story. I didn't

just wake up one day and decide, 'La la la, I'm gonna go find a new guardian.'"

Trident didn't look convinced. In fact, his smugness only seemed to increase.

"It's in the past," I said quickly, trying my best to defuse the situation before it exploded. "In any case, Checkers is now my aunt's familiar, and he's a fast learner."

Aunt Lavender beamed at her familiar, who looked shyly down at his fluffy paws. "He's also excellent at using the internet," she added.

Selene scoffed. "And yet somehow he couldn't help me order that aquarium I wanted last week," she muttered darkly, shooting Checkers a sidelong glower.

Checkers wriggled his hindquarters and bounded off, having found some sort of creepy crawly plaything.

Goddess bless him.

Trident still looked unsettled by our revelation, but after another moment of careful consideration, he spun back around and continued down the hall. He turned and passed through the open doorway of the second-to-last room on the right side of the hall. A large window stretched from nearly the ceiling to the floor, flooding the hallway with natural light and offering a glorious ocean view, peeking through the dense trailing vines that twisted and clung to the Juliet-style balcony.

The room was much like our own at the other end of the house. Two queen-sized beds dominated most of the space, their linens identical to those in our room. Both beds were rumpled, having clearly been slept in.

"This is Madeline's side," Trident explained, walking to the foot of the bed nearer to the window. "Her roommate, Alexandra, found her on the bathroom floor this morning when she woke up. That's the source of the scream you likely heard."

"Wait, Alexandra is Madeline's roommate?" Aunt Lavender glanced at me, then at Trident. "Not her sister?"

The sound of scampering paws echoed from the hallway, and Selene marched to the doorway, calling after Checkers. "Will you knock it off and get in here?" she scolded.

"Not anymore," Trident replied, his tone a little stiff. "Madeline and Ava may be twins, but they are not friends." He flicked his tail. "At least, not anymore."

"Why not?"

"To borrow your phrase, it's a long story. One even I do not know in its entirety."

"Ha. I doubt that," Selene quipped. "You seem like quite the busybody."

Trident's tail stopped swishing and his yellow-green eyes narrowed. "I don't get involved unless something directly impacts the Sisterhood. And, despite their personal upheaval, the two have managed to keep most of the drama away from these quarterly meetings. The bad blood between them doesn't impact the ritual, so I stay out of it. But suffice it to say, the two used to share a room, until about two years ago."

Aunt Lavender and I exchanged a look.

Selene was busy perusing the room, looking for any kind of clue. "Yep, looks like Charybdis lace to me," she said upon finding a bowl of soup that had been left on the small table along a row of windows overlooking the beach below. The narrow double doors to the small balcony were closed. An array of painted pots containing a variety of small plants stood in clusters on either side of the balcony, with some potting soil scattered across the tiles.

"And no one knows where she got the soup? Chef Eleni insists she would never touch canned soup," I said, running it by Trident for his reaction.

The cat laughed, the sound like gravel crunching under the tread of a boot. "I suspect she'd rather walk into the sea than be forced to prepare something that comes from a can."

"Even for a person who clearly got under her skin?" I said, raising an eyebrow in his direction.

Trident shook his head, his fur ruffling. "Not even then. She takes far too much pride in her work. And aside from that, I doubt very seriously Madeline would have even asked her for the meal. Not after their argument yesterday. Madeline isn't the type to—" He stopped short, his eyes shifting.

I frowned. "Isn't the type to what?"

Trident sighed. "She isn't the type to humble

herself. I haven't yet figured out where the soup came from, but I can assure you, the pantry is not locked, and therefore anyone could have prepared it. This wasn't Chef Eleni."

We continued searching a little longer, but no clues jumped out at us immediately. The two roommates kept the room neat, most of their belongings in the suitcases propped on luggage racks at the foot of each bed. There were no signs of foul play, and without knowing the origin of the poisoned meal, we were at a bit of a loss.

As we left the room a few minutes later, Aunt Lavender and I exchanged a look. "I think it's time we talk to Ava, and see if we can get down to the bottom of this family feud."

Lavender gave a sage nod. "Indeed."

10

The sun beat down on my shoulders as we trudged along the beach, our feet sinking into the warm sand with each step, and I wished I'd thought to ask someone for a bottle of sunscreen. Someone had stocked our bathroom with toothbrushes, toothpaste, and shower essentials, but I hadn't seen lotion or sunscreen anywhere. My summer tan was only just starting to fade, and I hoped it could stave off a nasty burn.

Selene padded along beside me, grumbling under her breath about the sand in her paws.

"You know, I'm surprised by you, Selene," Aunt Lavender said as she straightened, having paused to inspect an interesting bit of seashell.

Selene looked toward her, suspicion blossoming across her furry face. "How so?"

"You've gotten soft. Turned into a pampered indoor kitty." Aunt Lavender smiled.

Checkers snickered.

"What exactly did you expect, coming on such a trip? You and I spent months in Morocco, in the depths of that archeological dig site, and I don't recall you complaining so loudly."

I picked up my pace, desperate to get clear of the impending *boom*.

"What can I say, Lavender, it seems getting shipwrecked has made me a bit cranky," Selene replied, snark dripping from every word. "Back in Morocco, you had your wits a bit more about you, and I didn't have to worry about being turned into fish food!"

She cast a pointed glance toward the water, where silvery fins poked above the waves a few yards offshore.

Aunt Lavender flapped a hand in her former familiar's direction. "I wasn't about to let that happen."

"Oh, look, there's Ava," I said, grateful for the distraction as I pointed out a figure sprawled on a large beach towel a little ways up a small sand dune. The last thing I needed was for Aunt Lavender and Selene to take a bitter and winding trip down memory lane. Those conversations never ended well, and while the mansion and island surrounding it were decently sized, I had no doubt they would both feel cramped should the two of them go to war.

Ava lay on her stomach, the straps of her black bikini top untied to avoid tan lines. Her chin rested on her crossed forearms and a pair of oversized sunglasses perched on the tip of her nose as she scanned the glossy pages of a magazine. My sinking feeling about the woman only intensified at finding her so casual, like a woman on a well-earned vacation.

As we approached, Ava lifted her head, pushing her sunglasses up to rest on top of her head.

"We need to talk to you about Madeline," I said, trying to keep my voice neutral. Glancing down, I noted the magazine spread was filled with women in impossibly elegant wedding gowns. Ava's left hand was bare of an engagement ring, but perhaps she was a bride-to-be. Or maybe she just really liked weddings?

Ava's lips thinned into a tight line. "I've already told Althea everything I know, which isn't much. Now, if you don't mind, I'm trying to relax."

"Relax?" Selene scoffed, her tail lashing. "Your sister is fighting for her life, and you're out here working on your tan?"

Ava's face flushed, whether from anger or embarrassment, I couldn't tell. "You don't know anything about me or my sister," she snapped. With a snap of her fingers, the bikini tied itself back into place, and she sat up, glowering over her dark sunglasses. "So why don't you take your little detective act somewhere else?"

Selene's tail lashed back and forth. "Listen, you sunbaked sardine—"

"When did you speak with Althea?" I asked.

"This morning. Right after Alexandra found Madeline." Ava flipped the page of her magazine, showing a spread of up-close photos of the latest trends in engagement rings. "She told me about the plant in the soup. The whole thing is probably some kind of mistake. Madeline probably thought that lace stuff was some kind of fancy garnish. And believe me, if it's fancy, Madeline has to have it." She rolled her eyes before shoving her sunglasses back up the bridge of her nose. "Now, I'd appreciate it if you'd leave me alone."

Just then, a familiar voice spoke up from behind us. "I'm afraid that won't be possible, Ava."

We turned to see Trident padding across the sand, his fluffy tail held high like a banner.

"Trident?" Ava said, her voice still peppered with irritation. "Surely you're not encouraging this intrusion?"

The black cat sat down, his tail curling neatly around his paws. "I'm afraid I must insist you cooperate and answer their questions, Ava."

Ava's mouth dropped open. "You can't be serious. Why are you going along with this? They're outsiders. They have no right to—"

"Althea has given them her permission," Trident interrupted, his voice smooth but firm. "It is imperative we get to the bottom of this matter as swiftly as possible."

Ava's mouth opened and closed a few times, clearly

struggling to find a counterargument. Finally, she let out a long, exasperated sigh. "Fine," she huffed, slapping the magazine closed. She made a dismissive gesture with her hand, rolling her fingers in the air. "Get on with it, then. What do you want to know?"

I glanced at Selene, who looked far too pleased with this turn of events, then back to Ava. "Thank you," I said, trying to keep my tone neutral. "You don't really think Madeline put the Charybdis lace in her own soup, do you?"

Aunt Lavender frowned. "It seems unlikely something like that would be kept in a kitchen."

"I can assure you, it is not," Trident added.

Ava's lips pressed into a thin line, her eyes darting between us and Trident. "Fine, maybe it wasn't her doing, but I don't know who else would do something like that. I'm sure it was some kind of accident."

"So, you don't know anyone who would want to harm Madeline?" I asked.

"Like, oh, I don't know, perhaps yourself," Selene added.

I frowned down at her. "Would a teaspoon of tact kill you?"

This earned me a steely glower from both cats. Then Selene leaned over and used a stage whisper, "Not the best choice of words, Cora."

"Oh—" I blinked. "I just meant—"

"I didn't poison Madeline!" Ava interrupted as she got to her feet, her magazine abandoned in the sand.

She folded her arms as she rose to her full height. "I may not be crying at her bedside, but that doesn't mean I don't care, and it certainly doesn't mean I tried to hurt her."

"What happened between you two?" Aunt Lavender asked. "I have a sister. I know how it goes, sometimes, but this seems different. More serious than normal squabbling."

Ava hesitated, and for a moment, I thought she might refuse to answer, but she looked at Trident and sighed heavily. "It's ... complicated. We had a falling out two years ago."

"Over what?" Selene prompted, her tail twitching impatiently.

Ava's lips curled into a sneer. "Over her spectacularly bad life choices, if you must know." She paused, seeming to wrestle with how much to reveal. Finally, she continued, her voice tight with barely contained anger. "Madeline married for money. Some shipping tycoon twice her age. But when it all went belly up and ended in divorce, she was left with nothing."

"Yikes. Must have been one heck of a prenup," Selene replied.

Ava let out a bitter laugh. "Oh yeah. Iron clad. And Madeline, in her infinite wisdom, did the one thing that ensured she wouldn't have a claim to alimony or any type of settlement."

I arched one brow.

"She had an affair," Ava added, her tone deadpan.

"Some artist who moonlights as a bartender, and barely has a pair of coins to rub together. And for a woman like my sister, that's a real problem."

Selene's ears perked up at this. "So she came to you for help?"

"*Help* isn't quite the word I'd use," Ava replied, her lips twisting. "Madeline expected me to foot the bill while she looked for her next sugar daddy. And I did, for a little while, at least. She's my twin sister. I couldn't just let her starve. So, I let her stay with me, and helped her look for jobs. But Madeline..." She trailed off, shaking her head in disgust.

"What happened?" I prompted.

Ava's face hardened. "She refused to get a job. She would lie and say she was out at some job interview, but then I'd find out she was partying. She'd say she was going to a job fair or training, and then head out on some yacht, like a teenager sneaking out past curfew. And when I'd confront her about any of it, she'd just laugh and tell me to lighten up, or say she was 'networking.'" Ava scoffed. "All while I was footing the bill and dealing with complaints from the neighbors."

"What kind of complaints?" I asked.

"Noise, mostly. She'd come in late and stomp around. She had a bad habit of parking in reserved spots, too."

"That sounds frustrating."

Ava breathed a dry laugh and looked down at her

bare feet, halfway sunk into the loose sand. "That's a word for it. After six months, I kicked her out. Told her she needed to grow up and take responsibility for her life. She didn't take it well." She looked back up at us, her lips set in a firm line. "After I cooled down a little, I tried to reach out to her, to make sure she was safe, but she blocked me. And now, the only time we see each other is at these gatherings."

She looked toward Trident, and her voice took on a sharper edge. "Though I stand by my position that she is unqualified for her role within the Sisterhood."

Trident's tail flicked dismissively. "That is not how it works, Ava. You know this."

"I don't know why Althea can't change the rules. It seems unwise to keep a thief around."

"Thief?"

"Oh, yeah," Ava scoffed. "A few months ago, I discovered she went to my storage unit, dressed like me, and got one of the employees to open the unit for her. She took a bunch of the family heirlooms my mom left me. I'm sure they're long gone now, off to the highest bidder, so she could buy herself a Gucci bag or something."

"That's—that's awful, Ava. I'm so sorry that happened to you."

Ava bobbed her head, her gaze trained at her feet once again. "I didn't have room for them in my condo, but that didn't mean they weren't important to me."

"Of course," I said, sympathizing with her.

Ava squared her jaw and lifted her head. "So, yeah, you'll have to excuse me if I'm not acting the *right* way. I don't want Madeline to…" She trailed off, making a vague gesture. "I was angry with her. I've been angry with her. But I didn't have anything to do with this. I didn't poison her."

Aunt Lavender stepped forward, her voice gentle. "We're not accusing you of anything, dear. We're just trying to understand the whole picture."

Ava slipped her fingertips under her sunglasses and wiped at her eyes. "It's just … it's all so messed up. Madeline and I, we used to be so close. We're twins! And now…"

I glanced at Selene, seeing the wheels turning in her feline brain. This new information certainly painted Ava in a suspicious light, but her reaction felt genuine to me.

"Can you think of anyone else who might have a reason to hurt her?" I asked.

Ava shook her head. "No. But, like I said, we don't talk. And the other members know better than to bring her up around me. So, if she has issues with someone else in the Sisterhood, it's off my radar."

Selene and I exchanged a sidelong look. It seemed far-fetched that drama among such a small group could go unnoticed, but as I thought back to the night before, at dinner, Ava had seemed fairly isolated, rarely speaking with the women seated around her.

Trident, who had been quietly observing, finally

spoke up. "Thank you for your cooperation, Ava. I'm sure Althea will appreciate your candor."

Ava nodded stiffly, then gathered her towel and magazine and headed off down the beach. It was clear the interview was over.

I was left with more questions than answers.

11

*T*he grounds were strangely empty as we made our way back to the mansion. We found Mom on the deck, alone, the dishes and food cleared but for the mug in front of her. The steam billowing from the contents suggested Zora or Eleni was somewhere nearby, watching for signs of her needing a refill.

Checkers picked up his pace and jumped into Mom's lap.

"There you are," she said, scratching behind Checkers' ears. "I was beginning to wonder if you'd gotten lost."

"Lost? Ha! What kind of chowderhead do you take me for, Lilac?" Selene muttered, shaking sand from her paws. "Hmm. I could go for some chowder right about now. Something creamy and hearty, with extra fish bits!"

I rolled my eyes and took the chair across the table from Mom. "You had breakfast, cat."

"Isn't is lunch time?" Selene asked, blinking innocently.

"Not even close."

"Any progress?" Mom asked.

I shook my head. "Not really. I'd say we can tentatively rule out Ava."

"You do?" Aunt Lavender turned to look at me. She'd continued to the other side of the deck and was reaching overhead, investigating the blossoms of the hanging flowers woven through the pergola's rustic beams. "I thought she made the opposite case. She has a motive in spades!"

"But why now? And why here? Seems like it would have been easier to do back home."

"What's the motive?" Mom asked.

Selene gave her the abbreviated version.

Mom looked horrified when she finished. "That's awful! I couldn't imagine such a betrayal."

"Well, luckily for you, Lavender refuses to get rid of anything. So there is a zero percent chance she'd take your stuff and pawn it," Selene replied with a swish of her tail.

My aunt frowned in the cat's direction.

I tried to hide a smile as I leaned forward and rested my elbows on the edge of the table. "What about you, Mom? Did you learn anything while we were gone?"

Checkers adjusted his head and Mom continued

stroking under his chin. "Not much, I'm afraid. Everyone was pretty tight-lipped. But Daphne mentioned that when she got back from feeding Louka, she saw an empty soup can in the kitchen sink."

Selene's ears perked up at this. "She's one of the sea nymphs, right? The one we saw last night on the beach?"

Mom nodded.

"We have something of a timeline then," Selene continued. "They went off and did their little ritual thingy—which we still need to figure out—and then Daphne went to the kitchen to get the leftovers for the snake—"

"Serpent," I interjected.

Selene scowled at the correction. "She must not have seen the can in the sink beforehand, or else why bring it up? So, between the time she left and the time she got back, someone laced the soup with the Charybdis lace."

"How much do you really know about this plant?" I asked Selene. "It must be pretty slow-acting stuff, if she ate the soup last night and wasn't found until this morning."

"We would need to know how much she ingested. That bowl in the room looked like she'd hardly touched it. If she only took a few bites, maybe she didn't get very much of the lace. It might be her saving grace."

"I think we should talk to Alexandra next," I said.

"She was the one who found her this morning, and as Madeline's roommate, she might know if there was someone else who had a beef with her."

"Beef? Hmm." Selene swished her tail. "Nah. Never much cared for cow. Or cows, for that matter. I lost my second life to a runaway cow, if you can believe it!"

We all stared at her until she blinked. "What?" she demanded.

"Come on," I said with a little groan as I got up from my seat. "This little walk down memory lane will have to wait."

"Fine, but it's your loss. I've been told I'm quite the storyteller."

Aunt Lavender eyed Selene. "There's a difference between being told you're a good storyteller and being told you're full of—"

"Okay!" I said, getting to my feet. "Let's not start that again. There's enough tension on this island as it is."

WE FOUND Alexandra in the room she shared with Madeline. The beds were now made and the subtle scent of lemon clung to the air, even as an ocean breeze swept inside from where the balcony door was propped open. The slight, dark-haired woman sat at the writing desk by the window, bent over a leather-bound journal, a gold-plated pen in hand. She glanced up at our approach, her lips parting slightly as confusion worked its way across her delicate features.

Trident swished past Selene, and while he stopped just shy of tickling her nose with the tip of his tail, it seemed the tempting thought had crossed his mind. "These people need to ask you some questions about Madeline."

Alexandra looked at each of us in turn, questions in her dark eyes. "Okay?" she said slowly as she closed the journal and laid down her pen. It promptly rolled off the table and landed on the wood floor.

Mom swooped forward and retrieved it, then offered the woman a warm smile as she handed it back.

"Thank you," Alexandra said.

"I'm sure this has all been a bit of a shock," Mom continued, her voice taking on that soothing tone she'd perfected over years of dealing with scraped knees and hurt feelings.

If I had to guess, Alexandra was one of the younger members of the Sisterhood, perhaps only in her mid-twenties. At dinner the night before, she'd seemed shy and reserved among the other, stronger personalities. In a way, she was like Ava, just without the thick cloak of bitterness heavy on her slim shoulders.

"Is there any update on Madeline?" Alexandra asked, this time looking to Trident.

"Not yet."

Alexandra's lips pressed together and she gave a slight nod. "I keep thinking, maybe if I'd gotten up earlier. You know? Maybe I could have—"

"You can't think like that, dear," Mom gently interjected. She shifted, and I could tell she wanted to reach out and squeeze the young woman's arm to comfort her. "You did everything you could."

Alexandra didn't look convinced.

"How long have you been a part of the Sisterhood?" Aunt Lavender asked.

"Four years now," Alexandra replied. "Althea recruited me. I was studying environmental sciences in college—still am, actually—and I met her at an art gallery. I have a minor in studio art," she added, a small smile touching her lips for the first time.

"And Madeline and Ava? They were already members?" I prompted.

Alexandra nodded. "Yes, they've been part of the Sisterhood longer than I have. Their mother was a member, too, before she passed."

"Is that common?" I asked. "For it to run in families?"

"Sometimes," Alexandra said. "Althea says the goddess shows her who to pick. The Sisterhood is bigger than just the nine of us. A lot of the older members have moved on to other roles and duties. The ritual requires a large amount of magic, so it's best if—"

"Let's keep the conversation to Madeline," Trident interrupted. He gave Alexandra a look, and while it wasn't harsh or angry, it was firm. The young woman nodded, then reached for her pen and began twisting it between her fingers.

Selene glared at Trident, but thankfully kept any percolating threats to herself.

For now, anyway.

"What can you tell us about last night?" I asked. "Did you see Madeline after the, uh, ritual?"

Alexandra's gaze drifted to the empty bed across the room. "She was in bed when I got back to the room."

"And what time was that? Roughly."

"Um, maybe midnight. I was out with Thalia and Lydia. They might know the time for sure. We all walked back together after going up to the hot springs. It's kind of our tradition, or routine, I guess."

"Did you see the bowl of soup on the table?" Aunt Lavender asked, gesturing to where the woman now sat. I wasn't sure who had cleared it away. Perhaps Zora got a little overzealous in her cleaning.

Alexandra shook her head. "No, I didn't see anything like that. But I wasn't really looking, you know? It was late and I was pretty tired. I didn't even shower. I just got into bed, and figured Madeline had, too."

"I know this might not be a pleasant question to consider, but we're trying to figure out what happened to Madeline. Do you know anyone here who might have wanted to hurt her?"

Alexandra looked stricken. "What? No! Of course not."

"Are you sure?" Selene asked. "Because we've been here for about twenty-four hours now, and it seems she didn't really play nicely with others."

Alexandra frowned. "You mean Ava? They have their issues, sure, but Ava wouldn't do something like this."

"What about the others? Does Madeline have history with any of them?"

Alexandra heaved a sigh that somehow seemed too big for her body. "Look, I'll be honest and say Madeline isn't exactly my cup of tea. I didn't really want to be her roommate, but Ava begged me to switch places with her, and Ava's always been nice to me, so I agreed. I was also the newest member at the time—this was before Iris—and didn't really feel like I had much of a choice." She hitched a shoulder in a slight shrug. "I feel it's easier to steer clear of Madeline. If I stay out of her way, she doesn't notice me. And since Iris got here, that's been pretty easy. The two of them are thick as thieves, for whatever reason. On the outside, I'm not sure what they really have in common."

"Do the others feel that way, too, then? That it's best to steer clear of her?"

Alexandra considered the question for a long moment, her nails tapping absently on the leather cover of her journal. "I really shouldn't speak for anyone else. But I will say, I think we were all a little relieved when Iris came along and took Madeline's focus."

Suddenly, Selene's posture shifted. Her front half lowered down, her eyes intent and trained on the balcony door.

"What is it?" I asked.

Selene leaped into action, hitting the door with a blast of magic to throw it open wider before she bounded through.

"Selene!" I called, hurrying after her. "What in the world are you—"

"Look!" she exclaimed, her nose pointing to a scrap of pale blue fabric snagged on the pointed end of a twisted detail in the wrought iron railing. It flapped in the balmy breeze as I squatted down to look at it.

Selene peered over the side of the balcony. A trellis leaned against the house to allow the flowering vines to climb, unimpeded, to the second level of the estate. "Looks like someone was out last night doing a little free climbing."

I snared the fabric between two fingers and gently removed it from the railing. "It's the same color as the nightgowns Zora laid out for us." I ran the pad of my thumb over the subtle sheen. "The same fabric, too, if I'm not mistaken."

Selene flicked her tail toward me and swept the scrap from my fingertips with a wisp of magic.

"Hey!" I protested.

Not that she was listening.

She held the fabric over her head, engulfed in a cloud of magic, and marched back into the bedroom. "All right. I've cracked this case wide open!" she crowed. "The would-be killer was on this balcony last night. So, we just need to find out who has a tattered nightgown, and we'll have our culprit. Case closed."

"Okay, Matlock," I grumbled as I followed her inside.

Aunt Lavender clasped her hands together. "That's quite a find, Selene!"

Selene lifted her chin, her eyes nearly closing as she lavished in the praise of her former guardian. "Yes, yes. All in a day's work. Perhaps a bit of fish might be a suitable reward." She cracked open one eye and swiveled it in Trident's direction.

He twitched his whiskers, but didn't reply. Instead, he turned to Alexandra. "Alexandra, you need to open your closet."

12

"*W*ait, what? Trident, you couldn't possibly think I had something to do with this," the young woman protested. "Why would I need to climb around on the balcony, anyway? This is my room, too."

"It's a matter of principle," Trident clarified. "It's essential to the Sisterhood that everyone is held to the same standards. If I go around asking everyone to turn their closets inside out, I can't give you a pass."

I frowned, not sure I agreed with the cat's sentiment, at least not from a logical standpoint.

Alexandra rose without further argument and crossed the room to the wardrobe opposite the two queen-sized beds. The hinges creaked softly as she opened the doors, and Trident scowled. "Remind me to have Zora see to that," he said to no one in particular. "We can't have squeaky hinges."

Selene scoffed. *"That's* what you're worried about?"

Trident scowled at her but quickly twisted his face away and watched as Alexandra produced two identical nightgowns, both the same pale blue that almost looked iridescent in the early afternoon sun. Neither of them showed so much as a burst seam, let alone a large tear.

Satisfied, Trident gave a subtle nod and flicked his tail toward the wardrobe, indicating for Alexandra to close the doors. "Thank you, Alexandra. Now, I suppose we need to gather the others and have everyone gather and bring their nightgowns for inspection."

I cleared my throat and lifted a finger. "If I could—"

Trident twitched and stared up at me. "I realize we are guests here, and I'm not trying to tell you what to do, but I was just thinking that—"

"Oh, spit it out, Cora," Selene growled.

"I just think it might be better if we took a more subtle approach to the search. If you could keep everyone occupied, we could go room to room and find the torn nightgown without raising the alarm."

Trident considered this for a moment, his eyes taking on that distant look before he blinked three times in a row and straightened to his full height. "Very well. I will call a meeting. Althea wants to speak to everyone anyway. So, while I'm seeing to that, you may search the rooms."

Something about his tone made me think he wasn't

altogether comfortable with the idea. However, he seemed like the type to stick to his guns once he made a decision, so without waiting, he twitched his tail and turned to leave the room.

Just as he was about to turn the corner, Zora passed by, carrying a large wicker basket full of what appeared to be fresh towels, brilliant white and folded into a neat stack. Trident stopped short and let her know we'd be looking around, then took a few more steps before calling over his shoulder that she needed to grease the hinges on all the wardrobes.

Then he was gone.

Zora entered the room with a masked expression. She slipped into the bathroom and when she returned, the stack in the basket was a few towels short. She looked at us expectantly before heading back through the open doorway. "Come along. I'll show you to the other guest rooms."

"Do you need a hand with that?" Mom asked, gesturing at the laundry basket.

Zora looked horrified by the mere suggestion, all but flinching away.

"I just thought it looked heavy," Mom added with a shrug.

Zora's expression pinched. "I'm quite all right. Now come on. I'll be needed in the kitchen soon enough, to help Eleni with the afternoon tea service."

"Oh, how marvelous!" Aunt Lavender said, her eyes alight.

The first room Zora took us to belonged to Thalia and Daphne. Zora raised an eyebrow, but didn't question us as she went about her business of making the beds and restocking the towels in the adjoining bathroom. Aunt Lavender and Mom rummaged through the wardrobe and I glanced around the rest of the room. In contrast to the room Madeline shared with Alexandra, this room was quite lived-in, especially considering the women had only spent one night so far on the island. It seemed Thalia and Daphne were the types to make themselves comfortable almost instantaneously upon arriving in their temporary home.

The room had its own balcony, but instead of an ocean view, it looked out upon a courtyard with stone sculptures and neatly trimmed rose bushes. It struck me as odd that one of the sea nymphs would wind up with a garden view room, but then I wondered if perhaps she, too, enjoyed a change of scenery when she traveled to land.

"Everything looks good here," Aunt Lavender announced as she rehung a hanger with a nightgown.

Zora emerged from the bathroom and retrieved her basket from the floor. "I realize it's not my place," she began, hedging her words, "but if you're looking for something specific, perhaps I could point you in the right direction."

Mom, Aunt Lavender, and I exchanged a quick glance, coming to a silent consensus.

"We think whoever poisoned Madeline may have

accessed her room via the balcony. We found a scrap of fabric torn off and caught in the railings. So the idea is that whoever has a torn nightgown may also be our perpetrator."

Zora's olive-toned skin paled as the blood drained from her face. She muttered something in Greek under her breath, though I couldn't understand it.

Selene, on the other hand, could, and quickly looked up, intrigued. "I didn't catch all of it, but something about the 'sea' was involved."

Zora's eyes flashed with surprise and a flare of anger. "I've always told Althea that just because they belong to the sea doesn't mean they can be trusted implicitly. Especially not royal ones." She said this as though it were the darkest of curses.

"What do you mean? Who are you talking about?" I asked.

Instead of responding, the housekeeper pivoted on her heel and marched down the hall two more doors, pointing us toward a room, its door closed. "Iris," Zora said.

Without bothering to elaborate, she surged forward, abandoning her basket in the hallway before throwing open the door of the room. "It will be here somewhere," Zora said, already rummaging through the wardrobe.

"What makes you think—"

"Over here!" Selene exclaimed, wriggling halfway

under the bed. She re-emerged, dragging a nightgown with her teeth.

Zora leaned over and scooped the gown off the floor. Selene growled as the material caught on her canine and tore further.

"Watch it, lady! I have unlimited lives, not unlimited teeth."

I flashed a half-hearted smile. "I am always telling you about the benefits of flossing."

Selene glowered.

Zora inspected the gown, twisting the fabric to show us a large torn gash along the hem where the scrap had torn away.

"How did you know it was Iris?" I asked.

"She asked me for a sewing kit this morning. I told her to just give me whatever she needed mending—it's part of my job, after all."

"Did she say what happened?"

Zora shook her head, then scoffed in disgust as she ran her finger along the damaged fabric. "I didn't even know it was one of the nightgowns. She just told me she needed a sewing kit. And so I gave her one. I don't exactly get paid to ask questions."

Mom caught my eye, marking the tinge of bitterness in Zora's voice. I gave a small nod, letting her know I'd picked up on it, too.

"Well, looks like the case is closed!" Selene crowed, already strutting toward the door, her tail upright and aloft. "I can't wait to see the look on Trident's face when he realizes I was the one who got to the bottom of this. Ha!"

I frowned, a new question in my mind as I looked at the torn garment. "Zora, do you know why Iris would want to hurt Madeline? From what we've heard, the two of them are friends."

"Thick as thieves, I believe, was the expression used," Aunt Lavender added.

Silently, we all turned to Zora.

Zora dropped the tattered gown on the bed and straightened her plain black skirt, the fabric stretchy and breathable. "Madeline and Iris get along because they have one thing in common: they both think the world revolves around them."

My eyebrows lifted higher still, making a run at my hairline.

"Of course, that's largely Althea's fault. At least, in the case of Iris. She thinks it's quite a boon to have collected the eldest daughter of one of the most powerful lords of the sea."

"So she's nymph royalty?"

Zora's lip curled. "A princess."

I turned to Selene. "Didn't we see them going off together last night after she and Ava argued?"

"Who can say? They all sort of look the same, don't they?"

"Yes, there's that keen sense of observation you're always going on about," I said, rolling my eyes.

Selene bared her teeth.

"I really shouldn't be saying any of this—it's not my place," Zora said, though the look on her face suggested she very much wanted to tell us everything she knew, if only because she wasn't supposed to. "But I will say this: due to Ava and Madeline's difficulties, there's been some unrest in the Sisterhood. Every quarter, these meetings get more and more strained. It's disruptive, and if it continues much longer, it could cause serious rifts in the Sisterhood. And if that were to happen—" She stopped short, a bitter twist tugging at her thin lips. "Let's just say it would put the whole mission in danger."

I nodded, as it echoed something Trident had already told us. Granted, he'd been just as vague about the details. "So why not ask one or both of them to leave?"

"Oh, don't think that hasn't been suggested to Althea. But she can be particularly hardheaded about things. She personally selects everyone who joins the Sisterhood, and I think, in some ways, dismissing one would not only be unprecedented, but it would be admitting a failure on her part," Zora explained. "She says the members are chosen by the goddess, but we all know it's a pack of lies."

"Wow. And just how many times have you been made employee of the month?" Selene quipped.

Zora scowled and muttered something in Greek.

Selene flashed her teeth in a sardonic grin and matched her with an equally dark sounding reply.

Zora made a rude hand gesture and stormed out of the room, pausing only to yank the laundry basket from the floor.

"Way to go, Selene!"

Zora's footsteps echoed down the hall and faded as she rounded the corner.

"We don't need her," Selene replied. Then, with a lazy burst of magic, she levitated the torn nightgown from the bed and smiled. "We have the smoking gun!"

rident sat holding court on the covered deck, the flowering vines swaying gently overhead as the women gathered to get an update on Madeline's condition. We paused in the wide doorway, listening, and I noted Althea wasn't at the gathering. Dread roiled in my stomach, hoping her absence wasn't a sign that Madeline's prognosis had taken a turn for the worse.

While Althea was missing, it appeared everyone else had gathered—including Ava. She stood near the deck's railing, her back to the sea, listening to Trident with her arms folded over her chest. Despite the morning spent in the sun, she somehow looked pale and drawn.

"...and while it seems the treatment is helping to stabilize her, she has yet to show any signs of improvement or return to consciousness," Trident continued, only giving us the barest of glances. "Althea remains with her, monitoring her condition closely."

A collective murmur of concern rippled through the assembly. I scanned the faces, my eyes landing on Iris. The young sea nymph stood slightly apart from the others, her ethereal beauty somehow more pronounced in the golden light. One of the pink flowers from the overhanging vines was tucked behind her left ear.

Trident continued, his voice steady and authoritative. "We must remain hopeful."

The others nodded their agreement.

Satisfied, Trident slid a questioning glance in our direction, and I gave a small nod, confirming that we had indeed found something. His whiskers twitched almost imperceptibly in response. "It appears our guests have an update as well," he said, swishing his tail as if to beckon us fully from the shadows of the house.

"You know, I have a question," Selene said, striding forward onto the deck. "I've found the two-legged justice system leaves quite a bit to be desired, but what of that under the sea?" She swiveled a curious glance toward Daphne and Iris. "Have you nymphs got the whole thing figured out? Are there little underwater jails with reinforced kelp instead of iron bars? Oh! Or maybe well-trained electric eels as the fence to keep a perimeter in place. Of course, I suppose you could always go with sharks, too. They'd surely get the job done."

Trident's eyes flashed with irritation. "What are you babbling about?"

Selene stopped in front of Iris and peered up at her.

The nymph shifted back half a step before bumping into the deck's railing.

"Like I said," Selene continued, her voice a silky purr, "it was just a question. A little curiosity."

I sighed and marched out on the deck. "We think we know who poisoned Madeline's soup."

The reaction was immediate. Several heads snapped in my direction, eyes wide with surprise. Alexandra was the only one who didn't look stunned, though she'd had some advance notice on our mission.

"Oh, Cora." Selene scoffed. "Always stepping on my big moment."

"You were taking too long. We don't have time for you to play around."

"Don't we?" she asked, one ear cocked. "By my estimate, we have two more days of this fun."

"Who does the nightgown belong to?" Trident asked, his tail swishing agitatedly.

"Nightgown? What nightgown?"

I looked toward the source of the question. Sophia, Althea's assistant, stood in the corner, nearly concealed in the shade from the vines. She kept her tablet clutched to her chest. "We found a scrap of fabric, torn from one of the silk nightgowns, on the balcony outside Madeline and Alexandra's room."

Alexandra crossed her arms, looking almost sulky

as she shot suspicious looks at her fellow so-called sisters.

Aunt Lavender stepped out from behind me and held up the nightgown. "We found this under your bed, Iris."

All eyes turned to the young nymph, who looked like she might bolt at any moment.

"Iris?" Trident seethed.

The nymph's face crumpled. "It's not what you think!" she blurted out. "I didn't poison Madeline, I swear!"

"But you admit to being on the balcony last night?" I asked.

Iris wrung her hands, looking around at the expectant faces. "Y-yes. It was me."

A collective gasp went up from the group.

"But I ... I was trying to scare her," she hurried to add. "I swear!"

"Scare her?" Trident echoed, disbelief evident in his voice.

"It's a little early for a Halloween prank," Selene quipped. "I call bull! Or would minotaur be more culturally appropriate?"

"Selene," I groaned.

"What?"

Iris took a shaky breath. "It wasn't a prank. I wish it was something so silly."

"What the hell, Iris?" Ava demanded, pushing away from the railing to square off with the nymph.

"You of all people should understand!" Iris sputtered. "You know what she's like! She was going to sell us out! All of us!"

Another round of gasps and whispers ricocheted around the gathering until Trident smacked his tail against the table and a *boom* cracked like thunder.

Selene's eyes glowed. "Oooh. That was a pretty neat trick, furball! You might have to teach me before we go."

Trident barely spared her a proper glower before shifting his focus to Iris. "What do you mean?"

"You know how there's that weird collector guy who's been sniffing around, right?" Iris said, frustrated tears brimming in her eyes. "The one who wants to find Atlantis."

Trident swore darkly and thumped his tail again.

"Okay, Zeus, we get it," Selene grumbled.

"Yeah. Well, last night, after the ritual, Madeline and I split a bottle of wine. Or, er, maybe it was two. She got a little … chatty and told me about her money troubles and how she needed to pay her rent or she'd get thrown out and have nowhere else to go."

Ava rolled her eyes but backed off a step, no longer looking ready to strangle the nymph.

"It wasn't anything new, really. Three months ago, at our last meeting, she said most of the same things." Iris shifted a nervous glance around the circle. "But then she told me the collector had contacted her, and offered her a small fortune for the scepter—"

Trident made a hacking noise and shot a wide-eyed glance in our direction.

Iris crumpled in on herself.

"A scepter, huh?" Selene said, almost giddy at having discovered a new crumb of information. "What kind of scepter? Is it shiny?"

I shot a puff of air magic to ruffle the fur along her spine. "Not the time!" I hissed.

She shot me a dark look over her shoulder. "Speak for yourself!"

"It doesn't concern you," Trident said, his tail lashing back and forth, but stopping short of losing another peal of thunder.

"Obviously, I couldn't let Madeline do that, and when I tried to push back on it, she got annoyed and then tried to play it off like it was a joke, but I knew it wasn't. She didn't hang around much longer after that, but I couldn't stop thinking about it. And I thought if I could scare her with my dreamweaving magic, maybe she'd change her mind. You know, show her some dark, ominous sign."

"You should have come to me!" Trident hissed.

Iris nodded miserably. "I know it was wrong, but I didn't know what else to do. And I really thought it would work."

Ava huffed a derisive grunt and folded her arms, once more retreating to the furthest edge of the deck.

I frowned at Iris. Something wasn't adding up. "Maybe I'm just missing something here, but why did you have to climb onto the balcony to cast this, uh, dream spell?"

Iris glanced down at her hands, clasped and twisting together in front of her. "My magic isn't the best. I have to get close for it to work, and I didn't want to risk Alexandra getting caught with the nightmare, too. The balcony was the best place." She jerked her chin up, her eyes full of pleading. "But I swear, I had nothing to do with the soup! And in the end, I didn't even cast the dream spell."

"Why not?"

"I heard someone coming. I didn't want to get caught, so I scrambled down and ran off before they could see me. I think it was Sophia."

Iris glanced around the circle, but Althea's assistant was suddenly nowhere to be found. When had she left? And why?

Trident looked disgruntled as he made the same realization.

"I was in such a hurry I didn't even realize my nightgown got caught until I was back in my room and saw the tear. But I'll fix it!" she hurried to add. "I already got a sewing kit from Zora this morning."

"We know," Selene said, her tone almost bored. "How do you think we figured out you were the one with the rip?"

Iris blinked, clearly taken aback. "Zora turned me in?"

Selene started grooming her face. "Yeah, she doesn't

seem to be your biggest fan. Thinks you're a bit of a diva."

I rolled my eyes. "That's not helping."

"What time was all of this, exactly?" Mom asked. "Did you see Madeline in her room?"

"Good question!" I turned expectantly. "We know the soup was prepared sometime between Daphne leaving to feed Louka and returning to clean up the dishes."

Daphne gave a nod. "That's right. The can wasn't in the sink when I left, but it was there when I got back."

"And how long were you gone?" Mom asked.

Daphne considered this, then gave a gentle shrug. "Maybe twenty minutes. I remember it was eleven-eleven when I left. A lucky time!" She smiled, but it quickly faded. "So, it was probably around eleven-thirty when I got back."

"It was eleven forty when I got back to my room," Iris said. "I remember thinking at least I'd get to bed by midnight."

Across the deck, the dark-haired Lydia nodded. "I woke up when she came in."

Iris winced. "Sorry."

"It's okay."

"I really didn't mean for any of this to happen," Iris said, her sweet, almost melodic voice growing thick with emotion. A tear glistened on her cheekbone, the color silver and shiny, like the coating of a pearl. "She has to be okay. She just has to pull through. I'll apologize to her and make this right."

"And to Althea," Trident added.

Iris sniffled and bobbed her head fervently, sending another pretty tear splashing down her cheek. She wiped it away quickly, her mouth pulling into a miserable frown. "I just wish that Nell guy would go away. He's the one tearing us apart!"

My blood went cold.

Beside me, Selene, Mom, and Aunt Lavender all snapped upright like marionette dolls whose strings had just been yanked.

"What—what did you say?" I stammered, desperately hoping my ears were on the fritz. "*August Nell* is the one after this relic? This scepter?"

Aunt Lavender's hands balled into tight fists. "I know I should have turned him into a frog!"

Iris frowned. "I think so." She looked to Trident for confirmation.

"August?" the cat repeated, his eyes narrowing in our direction. "No. This guy is named Arthur. Arthur Nell."

Selene buried her face in her paws, muttering a string of dark curses under her breath.

"You know him?" Trident snapped.

My heart sank. "Unfortunately, yes."

14

"This has to be some kind of sick, cosmic joke!"

Selene hadn't stopped pacing since we'd returned to our room after a fruitless attempt at finding Sophia. "It's like, there we are, walking along, right as rain … and *wham!* Kersplat! Sayonara!"

"Um … minus the whole attempted-murder-investigation thing," I reminded her.

Mom emerged from the bathroom with a heavy sigh. "I know we should be polite, and go down to dinner, but I'm so exhausted. Honestly, Cora, I don't know how you and Selene keep up with these sorts of investigations back home." She lurched for the bed and dove into an unceremonial—and uncharacteristic— flop.

Aunt Lavender, on the other hand, was across the room, pacing with as much bound-up frustration as her former familiar, the two of them crisscrossing through the other's path. She tapped a finger against her lips, muttering incoherently every other turn.

"If only there were a way to get word to Tabitha," she said, mid-pivot. "She'd be our best bet for finding out exactly what Arthur knows. The cad! After everything she went through to help him, only for him to break her heart. And now this?!"

Selene scoffed. "Oh, spare me the pity party for poor Tabitha. You've had a soft spot for her from the beginning. It's illogical, Lavender!"

Aunt Lavender glared as the two passed in a figure-eight, Selene sweeping toward the window as she turned away. It was like watching one of those old clocks where little wooden people popped out from doors on either side, dressed in their Bavarian finest.

"It's called empathy, you miserable sourpuss."

"Sourpuss?!"

"Oh, goddess," I grumbled, falling onto the other bed and reaching for the nearest pillow to cover my ears.

"Will you two stop it!" Checkers cried from his place atop the dresser. His little voice carried surprisingly well in the room, despite its high ceilings.

Aunt Lavender and Selene continued to trade glowering stares, their pace unceasing, but at least the bickering stopped.

"I think we just need a good night's sleep," Mom

said. "Things will look better in the morning. They always do."

Aunt Lavender and Selene jerked toward her, and I gulped. They'd found a common enemy.

"Or," I said quickly, "we could go check out the library. Come on. Neither of you can resist old books. I'll bet there's thousands of them in there!"

Aunt Lavender's eyes flashed and I grinned.

Got her!

The cat, on the other hand, would take a little convincing.

"And afterward, we can go see if Chef Eleni has any more of that salmon dip from breakfast."

Selene canted her head, considering. "I know what you're doing," she said after a beat.

I smiled. "But you'll go along with it anyway, won't you?"

Scowling, she stalked across the room, her tail swishing as she made her way toward the door.

MOM OPTED TO STAY BEHIND, while the rest of us rallied and trooped off to the library. It was a grand, two-story room with a soaring cathedral ceiling and floor-to-ceiling bookshelves lining the majority of the walls on both levels, but for large narrow windows that let in shafts of natural light. The scent of old paper and well-oiled leather hung in the air and reminded me of the rare book section of Raven's Quill, the bookshop back home in Winterspell.

"Well, all we need is a talking clock and a flirtatious candelabra, and we'd be all set," Selene muttered. "I still can't believe you made me watch that whole movie with the twins."

I sputtered out a startled cough. "I'm sorry, *made you*?! Selene, when have I ever been able to make you do anything?"

She lashed her tail in the air. "I certainly didn't volunteer."

"Uh huh." I gave Aunt Lavender a sidelong glance and rolled my eyes.

"It's one of my favorite movies," Checkers chimed in, keeping pace with Selene. "I know all of the songs. Would you like me to sing my favorite?"

"No!" all three of us said in unison, startling the poor creature.

Checkers was sweet as a berry pie, but his so-called singing was enough to make your ears bleed.

We made it a few more steps before the mutterings of a woman's voice floated down from somewhere on the floor above. I turned in a half-circle, and stopped when I spotted Zora, standing with her back toward us, not far from the landing of the right staircase.

"...always dusting, cleaning, serving ... never good enough ... don't even get to eat with them..." She stretched upward, rising to the tiptoes of her sensible flats, a feather duster in hand as she stretched to clean a shelf of ancient-looking tomes.

I exchanged a glance with Selene before clearing my throat loudly. Zora startled, nearly dropping her duster as she whirled to face us. "Oh! I didn't hear you come in," she said, smoothing down her apron. "Is there something you need?"

"We just wanted to take a look around," I said. "We can come back later, though, since you're trying to clean."

Zora hurried down the stairs. "No, no. You go ahead. I can always—"

Her voice trailed off as the door at our backs opened and Sophia strode into the library, nearly crashing into Aunt Lavender. She glanced up from her tablet's screen at the last moment, narrowly avoiding the collision.

"What the—" she exclaimed, coming to an abrupt halt. "What are you doing in here? Does Althea know about this?" She seemed to direct this question toward Zora, who could only shrug.

Sophia scoffed. "Fine. I'll go and ask her myself."

"Trident told us we could look around the library," I said, my tone edged with irritation. "But actually, this is good timing. We had a few questions for you."

Ignoring me, Sophia dumped her tablet and bookbag onto a nearby table, then turned and glowered at the stone hearth. The huge fixture was framed by tall stained-glass windows, though the details were largely concealed by the heavy drapes that hadn't been fastened in the brass holders mounted to the wall.

"Why is it so dark in here?" she complained, yanking the drapes fully open. Swaths of sunlight filtered in as Sophia reared back and sputtered at the dust motes swirling in the air.

Her eyes narrowed as she turned to Zora. "For heaven's sake, when was the last time these drapes were cleaned?" she snapped. "They're filthy!"

Zora's jaw clenched. "I'll take care of it right away," she said, her voice tight with forced politeness.

"See that you do," Sophia replied dismissively. "And use the vacuum this time, not just that silly feather duster."

With a stiff nod, Zora hurried from the room, leaving us alone with Sophia.

"Well, aren't you just a little ball of golden sunshine," Selene scoffed, glowering up at the woman.

Sophia arched a brow in the cat's direction before looking between me and Aunt Lavender. "You need to leave Zora to her work. Surely you have better things to do with your time than go around bothering the help. The pool is quite nice this time of day. I suggest you make use of it and stay out of everyone's way."

Before I could formulate a diplomatic response, Selene spoke up. "Is that right? And here we thought you might be up for a little chat. Although, you did tell us not to bother *the help*, and I suppose that includes you, too. Being Althea's assistant, and all."

Sophia's face flushed. "I beg your pardon," she said, drawing herself up to her full height. "I am an employee, yes, but my duties are far more important than keeping toilets clean. I am Althea's right hand!"

"Of course," I said quickly, trying to defuse the situation. "We didn't mean to imply otherwise."

"Speak for yourself," Selene muttered.

"We just had a few questions for you, about last night."

Sophia's eyes narrowed. "What about it?"

"Iris thought she saw you in the courtyard, coming from the kitchen. As you've made it clear you're not responsible for dishwashing, it does raise the question of what you were doing."

"Getting a midnight snack, purrr-haps?" Selene added.

Sophia scoffed. "I was getting tea. Sometimes the salty air makes my throat a little scratchy. Is that a crime?"

From somewhere in the hall a crash sounded, the breaking of glass unmistakable.

Sophia swore and threw her hands in the air. "Honestly, why Althea doesn't throw her out on her rear end is beyond me!" she muttered, already stalking toward the door.

As Sophia's footsteps faded down the hallway, we exchanged meaningful glances.

Aunt Lavender clucked her tongue. "Well, she's about as pleasant as a UTI."

I blinked. "That was ... colorful."

Aunt Lavender shrugged.

Selene's tail twitched impatiently. "Are you just going to stand there and twiddle your thumbs? We need to see what's so important that she's constantly glued to that tablet."

I hesitated a moment, my gaze shifting nervously to the door. There was no telling how much time we had.

Selene, however, was not content to wait for my approval—which was nothing new—and leapt onto the table, one paw reaching for the device.

She smacked the dark screen with her paw, swearing in frustration when it didn't register her touch.

"Here," Checkers said, hopping up silently beside her. He laid his paw on the home button and the screen lit up.

Selene stared at him, open-mouthed.

Checkers lifted his chin, his fluffy chest puffing with a tiny bit of pride.

"All right, give me that," Selene muttered, swiping the device her way.

Unfortunately, her vigor was a tad on the heavy side, and the tablet slipped off the table. Checkers lunged to save it but managed to knock Sophia's linen bookbag onto the floor beside the tablet.

"Mother of Merlin, you two!" I hissed as the contents of the bag scattered across the marble floor.

"That was all Checkers!" Selene hissed, her tail puffing up in alarm.

"It was not!"

Sighing, I dropped to my knees and frantically gathered the strewn items. "Watch the door," I whispered urgently in Aunt Lavender's direction.

She nodded, her face taut as she positioned herself as our sentinel.

I scooped up a sleek silver pen, a compact mirror, and a small leather-bound notebook, then reached under a nearby armchair, where a small tube had rolled out of sight. My fingers scrabbled across the cool stone floor and snagged the slim tube. With a sigh of relief, I withdrew my hand, expecting to see a lipstick tube. Instead, I found myself holding a small, intricately carved vial. Inside, a delicate strand of silver floated in a clear, viscous liquid, glittering almost iridescent in the golden sunlight.

"What is this?" I tilted the vial, watching the contents shimmer and dance. It was oddly beautiful, like liquid starlight captured in glass.

Selene's gasp cut through the tense silence. Her blue eyes went wide. "Cora," she hissed, "that's—"

The sound of approaching footsteps echoed from the hallway, cutting Selene off mid-sentence. Aunt Lavender gestured wildly for us to hurry. "Someone's coming!"

My heart leapt into my throat, and I surged up from the floor. I shoved the mysterious vial into my pocket and hastily stuffed the remaining items back into Sophia's bag.

I had just managed to right the tote and tablet on the table when the library door swung open. Sophia strode in, her heels clicking sharply against the marble.

"Absolutely incompetent," she muttered, before stopping short at the sight of us. "You're still here?"

I forced what I hoped was a casual smile, acutely aware of the vial's weight in my pocket. "We were just leaving," I managed, my voice sounding strained to my own ears. "I think the pool idea sounds nice, right guys?"

"Do we have to?" Checkers asked. "I don't think salt water agrees with my skin, and I just took a bath after breakfast."

If looks could kill, Selene would have vaporized the young cat on the spot.

Fortunately for all of us, she had no such power.

I breathed an awkward laugh and shooed Checkers out ahead of me. "How about a snack then?" I offered.

We scurried from the library and waited until we'd turned a corner before I pulled the vial from my pocket and held it up to Selene. "Don't tell me this is—"

"It sure is." Selene nodded. "That's Charybdis lace."

I eyed the iridescent plant once more, then slipped the vial back into my pocket. "Looks like we're going to that dinner after all."

15

To our surprise, Althea was at dinner, seated at the head of the table, just as she had been on the night of our arrival. Her dark hair was pulled back into an elegant chignon, and she wore a gown of deep blue that seemed to shimmer like the sea at her back as twilight descended. The crown she'd worn at our first dinner was absent, but her regal bearing more than made up for it.

As we approached, the quiet chatter around the table died down, all eyes turning to us.

"Ah, there you are," Althea said, her voice carrying easily across the deck. "Please, join us. We were just about to begin."

We took our seats, but I couldn't ignore the weight of the vial in my pocket as I shifted and struggled to get comfortable. Aunt Lavender caught my eye and gave a tight nod. Even Mom, usually the picture of calm, looked tense as she smoothed her napkin over her lap.

Zora and Chef Eleni stepped onto the deck, each holding a large pitcher filled with water. With a look from Althea, they both paused on the sidelines.

"Before we start the meal," Althea continued, her gaze sweeping over the gathered women, "I wanted to give you all an update on Madeline's condition."

The air seemed to still, everyone leaning in slightly.

"I'm pleased to report that she's stable and showing signs of improvement. The treatment suggested by our guests," she inclined her head slightly in our direction, "seems to be working, as Madeline briefly regained consciousness."

Gasps and murmurs broke out, but Althea held up a hand for silence.

"Unfortunately, she wasn't able to answer any questions before she fell back asleep. But the fact that she woke at all is incredibly encouraging."

"At least she'll be able to tell us where the damned soup came from," Ava said, her shoulders slumped with the exhale of what appeared to be a sigh of relief.

Selene jumped into my lap, her tail dancing in my face as she planted her front paws on the table's edge. "As it turns out, we already figured it out. We know who poisoned Madeline."

This prompted a second wave of whispers and muttered questions among the women.

"Is that right?" Althea said. "Well, please share your findings. I think that's something we'd all like to hear."

Althea gestured for Eleni and Zora, and the two swooped in without a word, moving to fill the water goblets. As Zora reached for my glass, she tilted the pitcher too far forward, sending an icy rain onto Selene and my lap beneath her.

Selene yowled and dug her claws into my leg, prompting me to yelp.

"Oh dear!" Mom hurried to try and dab away the mess, while Selene swore darkly.

"I'm so sorry," Zora said, recoiling quickly enough to nearly slop a second time.

Selene shook off like a dog—not that I would dare to draw that comparison while her razorblade-edged-toes were still in striking range—and growled until Zora backed up another step.

"Would you like to go and change? I can bring fresh towels and robes until I can dry your clothes," Zora offered.

Frowning, I blasted my lap and Selene with an air spell. It wasn't perfect, but it went a long way toward repelling the worst of the mess. "It's fine," I told Zora over my shoulder.

"I won't let a little water stop my big moment," Selene added, taking her position on the table again. "After all, we wouldn't want to give anyone time to slip away and finish what they started." Her head swung around until she was staring at Sophia. "Isn't that right?"

Sophia blinked, confusion etched across her face as she looked over the rim of her water goblet. "Why are you looking at me?"

"If you ask me, you're one lucky witch. Sounds like you'll get away with an attempted murder charge, instead of the full enchilada." She paused, tilting her head. "Or whatever the Grecian equivalent would be. A full moussaka, perhaps?"

Sophia's confusion morphed into annoyance as she set her goblet aside. "Attempted murder? You're saying *I* tried to poison Madeline? That would be insane."

"Oh, is that right?" Selene purred, her tail swishing as she turned toward me. "Cora, why don't you hit her with the facts?"

I couldn't help but roll my eyes at Selene's theatrics. Sometimes I wondered if she missed her calling as a courtroom drama star. Nevertheless, I reached into my pocket and pulled out the small vial.

"We found this in your book bag, Sophia," I said, holding up the vial for everyone to see. The botanical within shimmered ominously in the fading evening light.

"That's Charybdis lace," Althea confirmed, her expression going stony as she looked at her assistant.

Sophia's eyes widened, her face draining of color as she stared at the vial in my hand. "You couldn't have found it in my bag. That's ... that's impossible," she stammered. "And what were you doing going through my things, anyway?!"

As Sophia's voice rose in pitch, her hands began gesticulating wildly. "Althea," she pleaded, "this wasn't me. You know me. Why on earth would I try to poison Madeline? I have no reason to want her harmed!"

"Oh, I don't know," Selene drawled. "Maybe you just really hate her taste in shoes."

"This isn't some kind of joke!" Sophia snapped.

Suddenly, Ava's cool voice cut through the tension. "Perhaps it wasn't her own idea." Her gaze slid deliberately to Althea. "Maybe she was just following orders."

The accusation hung in the air for a moment before the table erupted in a cacophony of outraged voices. Daphne and Iris looked particularly scandalized, while Thalia and Lydia exchanged worried glances.

Althea, however, seemed unfazed by the accusation. She calmly raised a hand, and the table fell silent once more. "Ava, it seems you have something to say. Please, elaborate."

Ava leaned forward, her eyes never leaving Althea's face. "I've come to you at least a dozen times, trying to get you to cut Madeline loose from the Sisterhood. Every time, you told me it's a position for life." Her lip curled slightly. "And now, with Iris's confession that Madeline was planning to betray us all, well ... maybe you decided you wanted Madeline out of the Sisterhood for good but didn't have the heart to do it yourself. Or maybe you couldn't. Maybe that's baked into the vow. Either way, we all know if you snap your fingers, Sophia comes running."

Sophia balked, but wisely kept her mouth shut as she deferred to Althea.

Althea raised a single, elegant eyebrow. "You think I knew about Madeline's plans to betray us?"

Ava scoffed. "I think there's very little that happens on this island without your notice."

As the tension ratcheted up another notch, I noticed movement from the corner of my eye. Eleni had left the deck area, presumably to return to the kitchen, but Zora stood rooted in place, the pitcher of water in her hands wavering as her hands shook.

My eyes narrowed in her direction, something scratching at my brain.

"I can assure you, Ava, I would never harm a fellow member of the Sisterhood, and I do not believe Sophia was behind this attack, either," Althea explained.

"How can you be sure?"

Trident emerged from the shadows near a trio of potted plants. "Because Sophia was with me and Althea at the time of the poisoning."

"How do you know that?" Ava asked.

"We narrowed it down to happening sometime between eleven and eleven-thirty," I interjected.

Daphne nodded. "It happened while I was feeding Louka."

"And Sophia was with me and Trident in my office,"

Althea said, her gaze fixed on Ava. "I did not do this. I would *never* do this."

Ava held the woman's gaze for a beat, then looked down with a small nod. "I'm sorry. This has me rattled. I wasn't thinking straight."

"So, someone planted the lace in my bag?" Sophia exclaimed, suddenly shrinking back in her seat as her eyes shifted from face to face. "Why? Why set me up?"

Suddenly, Alexandra gasped, her eyes wide with horror. "Oh my goddess ... I just remembered..."

All eyes swiveled to the young woman as she struggled to get her words out.

"This morning, at breakfast," Alexandra continued, her voice shaky, "Sophia snapped her fingers at Zora, telling her to fetch her bag from her room."

Daphne and Lydia nodded. "She did! She used the word *fetch*, like she was talking to a dog," Lydia added.

The sound of glass shattering was followed by frantic footsteps as Zora bolted.

"Not so fast!" Trident's eyes glowed an eerie green and with a flick of his tail, ribbons of shadowy magic burst forth, chasing Zora as she tried to escape into the house.

With a jerk of his head, Trident pulled the blue-and-black ribbons back toward him, and Zora floated onto the deck, suspended in the strange shadows. She struggled and flailed against her bonds, but the cat's magic-enhanced grip held.

Althea rose to her feet, her presence suddenly

seeming to fill the entire deck. "Enough of this, Zora. It's time for the truth."

Zora writhed in her magical prison, her face reddening with effort and fury. "Let me go, you pompous—"

"The truth, Zora," Althea commanded, her voice resonating with power.

Something in Zora seemed to snap. Her struggles ceased, and a look of pure, unadulterated rage took over her features. "Yes! Fine! It was me!" she spat, her words dripping with venom. "And the only regret I have is that I didn't use enough of the lace!"

A collective gasp went up from the group. Even Selene seemed stunned into silence.

"But … why?" Iris asked, her voice small and confused.

Zora's bitter laugh cut through the air like a knife. "Why?!" Her eyes blazed as she looked around the table. "I'd think it would be quite obvious to anyone with ears! All of us, having to listen to that little witch go on and on. Whining and complaining, always making my life hell over the pettiest things. 'The sheets aren't soft enough, Zora.' 'The windows aren't clean enough, Zora.' 'Can't you do anything right, Zora?' She's a vampire! She sucks the life from all of us! You can all pretend to be sad that this happened, but none of you can say you've missed her today, not with a straight face!"

Her gaze swung to Sophia. "And you're no better!

Snapping your fingers, treating me like I'm less than nothing. Well, I thought I'd kill two birds with one stone. Take out the biggest thorn in my side and frame the second biggest."

Althea's face was a mask of disappointment and anger. "Zora, do you realize what you've done? The Sisterhood's purpose is bigger than this. It is imperative we stick together, no matter our differences or grievances. You've violated the sacred vows we all made."

Zora sneered. "Sacred trust? Don't make me laugh. There's nothing sacred about being treated like dirt."

"I am sorry you've felt that way, and clearly for some time. But you've left me with no choice. I expect Madeline will make a full recovery, but there will be justice."

With a nod toward Trident, Althea dismissed the woman.

Trident's eyes still glowed bright green as the magic held. The shadowy bonds morphed and changed, twisting Zora's arms behind her back and sealing her wrists together like metal handcuffs.

Silently, Daphne and Thalia got to their feet and approached Zora. She'd gone silent, but the hatred shone in her eyes as the two women took each of her elbows and began to march her away. Trident followed, keeping the magic in place.

A tense silence stretched as their footsteps faded. My stomach twisted and churned, reflecting how unsure I felt about any of it. Relief seemed wrong, somehow.

After a long moment, Althea turned to us, her expression grave. "It seems we owe you a debt of gratitude for helping to uncover the truth." She paused, her gaze sweeping over each of us in turn before continuing, "Ask for a boon, and it shall be granted to you."

The offer hung in the air, heavy with possibility. I glanced at Aunt Lavender and caught the spark of an idea dancing in her eyes.

Selene nodded in her former guardian's direction. "This one is all you, Lavender."

Aunt Lavender straightened in her seat and met Althea's eyes. "We wish for you to tell us what you know of Atlantis."

A collective gasp went up from the remaining members of the Sisterhood. Althea's eyebrows rose slightly, but she didn't seem entirely surprised by the request.

"Ah," she replied, a hint of amusement in her tone. "I should have expected such a request." She hesitated, then inclined her head in my aunt's direction. "Very well. It seems the time for secrets has passed. But first, you must make a sacred vow."

16

*S*elene was the first to speak. "Uh, what kind of vow are we talking here, lady? If it involves blood, chicken feet, eye of newt, or any kind of organ meat, I'm not interested."

Althea chuckled softly. "I assure you it is nothing of the sort. There is a simple binding spell—"

"Eh, we're not too keen on those, either," Selene interrupted.

I nudged her in the side to shush her.

Althea remained unruffled. "It is the Sisterhood's duty to protect Atlantis, and guard her many secrets. In order for us to tell you anything, you will need to swear to keep her secrets as well."

Aunt Lavender nodded. "I see."

Althea canted her head to one side, considering us in earnest. "Many seek the so-called Lost City, but they do so for their own personal gain. In you, I do not see such a dark motive."

"I assure you, Althea, my quest has never been about personal gain. Throughout my life, I've sought out many mysteries and adventures, and my travels have taken me all over the globe. It may sound trite, but I seek out impossible quests for the thrill of the hunt and, I suppose in no small part, to satisfy my own curiosity. The journey itself, the knowledge gained—that has always been my true treasure."

Mom nodded in agreement. "It's true. She's been like this since we were children."

"You should see her house," Selene added. "If she were in this for the money, she'd have a proper castle by now, instead of an overstuffed bungalow. And believe me, I've tried to corrupt her to the dark side. It just never took."

Althea smiled, a knowing look in her eyes. "I suspected as much. Your actions here have shown your true character."

Aunt Lavender inclined her head. "Thank you."

"Are you all willing to swear to keep the secrets of Atlantis, to protect them as we do?" Althea asked, looking at each of us in turn.

We agreed and Althea nodded, satisfied. "Very well. Please, join hands—and, well, paws—with the sisters."

We moved to form a circle with the other members of the Sisterhood. I felt a slight tingle as I clasped hands with Iris on one side and Thalia on the other. Checkers and Selene did their best to stay upright as they balanced on their hind legs so the sisters on either side could gently take their front paws.

Althea began to speak, her voice taking on a rhythmic cadence that seemed to swirl and stir the balmy ocean breeze. The hanging vines swayed with the magic of her words, filling the space with the delicate fragrance of the lush blossoms.

"BY THE DEPTHS of Poseidon's mighty realm,
   By Amphitrite's most sacred helm,
   We bind these hearts, these minds, these souls,
   To hold our secrets, to guide our goals.

LET TRUTH BE SPOKEN, let wisdom shine,
   Whilst Atlantis's purpose remain divine.
   So mote it be, by moon and sun,
   Our vow is spoken, our oath is done."

AS THE FINAL WORDS FADED, I felt a warm pulse of energy flow through our joined hands. It was gentle but unmistakable, like a wave washing over us.

The vines overhead went still once more as Althea opened her eyes. "It is done. You are now bound to the secrets of Atlantis, as we are. You will be unable to tell anyone of what you will see in the fathoms below."

Aunt Lavender's eyes sparkled with excitement. "You're taking us to Atlantis? Now?!"

Trident padded onto the deck and lifted his nose, sniffing at the air with a curious, if not suspicious, expression.

"Is Zora secured?" Althea asked her familiar as he came to stand beside her.

"Yes."

"Very well. Then you can come with us."

"Where are we going?"

Althea smiled and gathered the skirt of her gown as she stepped out from behind the table. "We're taking our guests to see Atlantis."

Trident balked, his tail fluffing to nearly twice its size. "We're *what*?!"

ALTHEA LED us up a winding path to the highest point on the island. Olive and cypress trees swayed gently in the balmy sea breeze, carrying with it the scent of wild thyme and oregano. The sun was still setting on the horizon, painting the sky with orange and pink hues, while birds made their way home to wait for its return.

"This way," Althea said, gesturing with the tip of a golden scepter toward a craggy crevice in the rock ahead.

A shiver skittered up my spine as we entered the cave. From the outside, I'd expected a dark and damp cavern, but instead the air was sweet and fresh, and glowing orbs bobbed along the top of the smooth stone, sending prisms of pale blue light bouncing off the surface, like dozens of glittering fireflies, there to light our path. The sound of running water echoed off the stones, coming from somewhere in the near distance.

"I still think this is most unwise," Trident hissed, keeping pace with Althea a few yards ahead.

"Yes, yes, your objections have been noted," Althea replied.

"You know, you two really do have a lot in common," I said to Selene.

She grimaced. "Watch it, Cora."

Mom and Aunt Lavender stifled a laugh. Checkers was up ahead, chasing and batting at one of the low-hanging orbs of light. Selene scoffed at the younger cat's antics. "So embarrassing. Lavender, can't you do something about your charge?"

"Oh, he's just having fun."

"Watch your step," Althea called back as she turned the corner.

We followed and began a sloping descent down a winding staircase. The stones beneath our feet were smooth but the steps were not perfect or uniform in nature, suggesting they'd been carved by centuries of rushing water rather than tools or machines. The air became cooler and damper as we descended, while the sound of flowing water grew louder and louder.

Eventually the source came into view and the stone steps disappeared under an inch of water, then two, then three, until it reached the middle of our calves. Selene, who had been padding along beside me, started to climb up my body, her claws digging into my clothes until she scrabbled up onto my shoulder and perched like a parrot.

"No one said we were going for a swim," she grumbled into my ear.

Althea turned back to us, an amused smile playing on her lips. "I was only testing your resolve," she said with a chuckle.

Before Selene could retort, Althea raised the scepter and spoke an incantation in Greek, her voice resonating with power. To our amazement, the water before us began to peel away, forming a tunnel around us.

"Come," Althea said, her voice filled with pride and excitement. "Atlantis awaits."

Mom and Aunt Lavender stared overhead, their mouths open, as they watched the water flow and bend around us.

At the end of the tunnel the staircase ended, and we found ourselves on a vast underwater mezzanine surrounded by water on all sides, appearing to be held back by ornate stone railings.

And ahead, the lost city of Atlantis.

Aunt Lavender sucked in an emotional gasp, the air hitching in her throat as she pressed a hand to her mouth. Mom whispered and hurried to join her sister —or perhaps keep her from diving into the water to get a closer look.

The city sprawled ahead, illuminated with an otherworldly glow in the dark blue depths of the sea. Towering spires of opalescent stone rose from the ocean floor, their surfaces shimmering like every stone and brick was overlaid with gold. The homes and buildings were capped with domes, each their own mosaic and work of splendid beauty. Wide boulevards formed pathways between graceful strands of kelp and clusters of stone and coral and fields of underwater botanicals.

Schools of brightly colored fish darted through the water like living confetti, while larger sea creatures meandered peacefully along the thoroughfares.

"Look!" Mom gasped, pointing to a pair of golden dolphins playfully weaving through the city's towers.

"Ah, those would be Amphitrite's most beloved companions," Althea said.

"They're beautiful," Mom breathed, entranced by the pair as they swam into the swaying kelp forest.

Aunt Lavender's eyes were wide with wonder as she traced the path of a massive manta ray gliding gracefully over the city's central plaza. "It's more beautiful than I ever imagined. I don't know why, but I thought of it as something of a dead city. Lost, I suppose, as the lore paints it. But it's so vibrant and alive!"

Althea gave a proud nod.

Sea creatures weren't the only inhabitants. A gathering of sea nymphs was tending to gardens of green vegetation, while others swam along the roads and moved behind the windows of the city's many structures. They were different than mermaids, with fins on the sides of their faces and hips, as well as along their powerful tails, but the effect was every bit as magical and enchanting as the stories of mermaids I'd adored as a little girl.

"Uh oh..." Selene's voice trailed off, her whiskers quivering as she tracked an approaching shadow spreading across the ocean's floor.

"There's my little sausage!" Althea exclaimed, waving as the shadow swirled and an enormous sea serpent descended toward us.

I swallowed hard, now truly able to gauge the creature's size. His scales gleamed like polished armor, flashing blue and silver as he moved closer. He grazed along the barrier of water and air surrounding the mezzanine like a bubble, but Althea reached out and broke through, water spraying softly as she let her fingers run along the serpent's side.

"Louka keeps watch over the city, too," she explained, still smiling like a proud mother as Louka swam off to explore.

"How ... nice," Selene said.

"As I alluded to before, the Sisterhood was formed to protect Atlantis. It is our duty to Amphitrite, the mother of this legendary city. It was given to her as a gift from her husband, god of the seas, Poseidon. As you may already know, he was not always faithful to his wife. His dalliances with mortals and nymphs alike caused his queen great pain. In an attempt to make amends, he created this," she gestured to the sprawling underwater metropolis, "as a gift to Amphitrite."

Althea's eyes seemed to reflect the shimmering lights of the city as she continued. "I do not claim to know the queen's heart, or whether she forgave Poseidon, but she accepted the gift and chose to make the city a sanctuary not only for herself, but also for those she chose to protect.

"As millennia passed and the world above changed, Amphitrite realized that keeping Atlantis hidden would require more than just her divine power. The prying eyes of mortals, armed with ever-advancing technology, threatened to uncover and exploit her precious jewel. That's where my ancestors came in," Althea said, a note of pride in her voice. "The island and Athánatos House became a safe haven for women accused of witchcraft and other perceived transgressions through the centuries, and my family cared for them, in addition to keeping Atlantis concealed."

Aunt Lavender smiled. "And thus, the Sisterhood was born."

Althea nodded. "Indeed. We gather every three

months, when the moon is full and our magic is at its peak, to renew and reinforce the wards and charms that keep Atlantis hidden from the world above."

"The ritual," I breathed, understanding dawning.

"Yes," Althea confirmed. "Each ritual strengthens the veils that shroud Atlantis, bending light and confusing mortal instruments. It's a delicate balance of magic and nature and requires the combined power of nine sisters."

"Huh. Nine. Sort of like The Muses." Selene sat listening intently to Althea.

Althea smiled. "You know your legends."

"You could say that." She twitched her tail. "So, what happens if you miss one of these little magical tune-ups, the whole thing comes crashing down?"

Althea turned her eyes toward the city. "Not immediately, but yes. Without regular renewal, the protections would eventually fade. That's why our commitment is so crucial, and why we can never allow outside interference. Or as is sadly the case in this most recent turn of events, inside interference."

A long silence stretched, and as I stood there, staring at the thriving city beyond, I understood why Althea and the others took their duty so seriously. They weren't just protecting a secret; they were preserving an entire world and a legacy that stretched back to the time of gods.

"What will happen to Zora?" I asked.

I couldn't imagine there would be a way to involve the Grecian authorities in the matter.

Althea's smile faded. "That will be a matter for the Sisterhood to decide. The larger group gathers more infrequently, but we will call a special assembly to determine the best course of action. The same is true of Madeline's future within the Sisterhood. We may need to make some larger changes, as much as that saddens me."

The reply only unleashed a dozen more questions, but the set of Althea's jaw told me it might be best to let it go.

"And what of Arthur Nell?" Mom asked.

"Oh, I think we can handle him," Selene interjected. "I'm sure Tabitha would sell him out. She's his ex-girlfriend, and I get the sense she wants her pound of flesh, too."

"There will be no need for that," Althea replied. "Although, before you leave tomorrow morning, perhaps we can compare notes on the matter."

Aunt Lavender smiled. "That we can do."

EVENTUALLY WE MADE our way back to the surface and found night had fallen over the island. The sisters who had accompanied us said goodnight and went their own ways, wandering back toward the mansion in twos and threes. The moon was still full enough to cast a good amount of light over the gentle waves, making for an easy walk back across the sand.

When we reached the steps leading up to the mansion's front door, Selene hung back, seemingly hesitant to go inside. Mom looked over her shoulder when I broke pace with her, and I gave her a nod, signaling she should go on ahead without me.

"Everything all right?" I asked once Althea, Mom, and Aunt Lavender were out of earshot. "You're not up to something, are you?"

Selene plopped down in the sand, her eyes trained on the cresting waves. "No, just thinking."

"Okay…" I lowered myself to sit with her and pulled my legs into a crisscross underneath me. "Is it about the bonding spell? I was sort of surprised you didn't ask Althea about it. Although I suppose we still have a bit of time."

"No. It's not that."

I chewed the corner of my lip, trying to decide what angle to try next, or if I would be better off leaving her alone.

After a moment, Selene spoke, though she didn't look toward me. "I made a discovery today, and it's changed the way I see things."

"I don't think you can take full credit for *discovering* Atlantis, Selene. It was kind of a group effort."

"I wasn't referring to Atlantis."

I bobbed my head, though I had no idea what she was talking about.

"We can talk about it when we get back home," Selene said abruptly. "I imagine you're happy we'll be allowed to leave tomorrow. Though I'm still not sure how we're supposed to get back, seeing as how our boat is still capsized. I swear I saw that sea serpent playing with it this afternoon, like it's some kind of rubber ducky for his bathtime entertainment." She scoffed and shook her head.

There were no signs of the serpent now.

"Althea will probably send us with the others through one of the dry portals back to the mainland. Though the boat is a problem. Let's hope the owner will take a credit card. Not sure how I'll explain that one to Clint, but let's hope he'll be so relieved to finally hear from me that he'll forgive and forget."

Selene flicked her tail. "Oh, I have no doubt."

I glanced over at her, unsure where her thoughts were, but it was clear she wasn't in a chatty mood. So I pushed up from the sand and brushed off the backs of my legs. "See you inside?"

"I'll be in shortly."

I looked out at the moon for a long moment, then turned and began to climb the stairs.

"Has anyone seen my gold bracelet?" Mom asked from her place on the floor as she kneeled to peer under one of the two queen-sized beds in our hotel room.

Thankfully, after our unexpected island detour, we'd managed to find a hotel in Santorini with room for us all. Three days had passed since our surreal trip down to the depths of Atlantis, and I still couldn't quite believe it had all been real. Of course, most of all, I was relieved to finally call Clint and explain everything.

"Did you check the shower drain?" Aunt Lavender asked, not looking up from her travel journal. She'd spent much of the past few days scribbling away, filling page after page, though if anyone got near, she turned cagey and secretive.

Mom grunted an acknowledgement as she swept a hand under the bed.

Selene scowled from her perch atop the dresser. "Oh, Lilac, think of all the filth under there."

"I'll check the bathroom," I said, abandoning my packing.

"Oh, are you sure, Cora? What if Clint texts and you don't immediately write him back?" Selene asked in a hurried tone, thick with feigned worry. "He'll surely perish!"

"I think you might just be jealous that Cora has someone waiting for her at home," Aunt Lavender interjected. She glanced over the top of her spectacles long enough to gauge the reaction of her former familiar. "The whole of Winterspell likely threw a parade when they heard you'd be going out of town for three weeks!"

Selene's eyes flashed as her tail lashed the side of the dresser. She hadn't yet mastered Trident's clap-of-thunder trick, though it wasn't for a lack of trying.

"Oh, and I'll suppose you're expecting a welcoming committee, then?" Selene asked. "Your neighbors and the head of your HOA were probably hoping you'd stay gone this time, and that someone else would buy the house. Someone who cares about watering the grass and pulling the weeds and doesn't terrorize the local children with tales of flesh-eating scarabs."

Aunt Lavender pointed her pen at the cat. "That was a public service announcement, and you know it! People don't talk about flesh-eating scarabs enough."

Mom groaned and got to her feet. "Okay, the next person who says *flesh-eating* is buying dinner."

Aunt Lavender and Selene glowered, like a pair of cowboys meeting at dawn with dueling pistols.

"What happens if I say it?" Checkers asked, his expression crumpled. "I don't have a wallet."

Selene swiveled toward the young cat. "As the

saying goes, don't write a check with your mouth that your body can't cash."

Checkers cocked his head. "I don't have checks, either."

Aunt Lavender frowned. "That didn't even make sense, Selene."

Selene *thwapped* her tail. "It made a perfect amount of sense. You would realize that if you weren't so busy scribbling away over there. What are you working on, anyway?"

With a smile, Aunt Lavender set down her pen. "I'm so glad you asked."

"I've been asking for days!"

"After speaking with Tabitha, I've decided to write a book."

Selene's eyes narrowed. "You've never wanted to before."

"Well, she's changed my perspective. We're actually discussing being co-authors, if you can believe that."

Selene choked on a hairball.

"Easy, there," I said. "Co-writing with Tabitha? What would the book be about?"

"The balance between seeking to uncover the secrets of myth and lore, and the preservation of the magic world. She's very upset about Arthur's betrayal. After everything she did for him."

"Wait. You didn't tell her about Atlantis, did you?"

"No. Of course not. I told her I got the tip off from a fellow adventurer on the trail for Atlantis.

According to Tabitha, Arthur got greedy and decided to take up where his brother left off, and when she didn't want to go along with his plans—which she suspects were being funded by big brother August—he got quite nasty and it ultimately led to their bitter breakup."

Selene rolled her eyes. "Oy. What a soap opera."

I chuckled to myself and went into the bathroom, determined not to be the one responsible for the dinner tab. It was our last night in Santorini, and personally, I was prepared to order the most expensive thing on the menu and wash it down with a bottle of whatever the server recommended.

It took a few minutes, but I found Mom's lost bracelet underneath her half-packed toiletries bag, and shook my head as I carried it out to return to her.

"All right," I said, clasping my hands together after helping Mom secure the bracelet around her wrist. "Last night in Greece. Should we head out? Our reservations aren't for an hour, but a little walk before dinner might be nice."

Selene cleared her throat. "There's one thing I need to say before we go. I have something of an announcement to make."

Aunt Lavender, Mom, and I exchanged wary glances.

"Okay," I said slowly. "What is it? And if this is about riding in the carrier on the flight back, it's not up for discussion. The airline makes the rules."

"While I stand by all of my previous statements on that matter, I had something else in mind."

My brows furrowed, though I didn't fully believe her. Selene never dropped things entirely. It wasn't in her nature.

"I've reached a decision about the bonding spell," she continued.

My brows rebounded and shot halfway up my forehead. "Oh...?"

"I've had quite a bit of time to consider my options since our unfortunate encounter with Mirin. I'll admit, there was a part of me that held out a sliver of hope that finding Atlantis might be the key to suspending time long enough to slip the bond, what with it being steeped in such old magic and all, but I've had a change of heart. And so—"

"Selene, you don't have to—"

She shook her head. "Cora, please."

My lips pressed together, and I offered a tiny nod.

Her ethereal blue eyes swiveled toward Mom. "As lovely as your grandchildren are, Lilac, I have no interest in becoming the familiar to Ruby or Emme whenever this one kicks the bucket."

Mom looked from Selene to me, worry etched into the lines of her face. "What are you saying?"

Selene looked at me and raised her chin. "I've decided that Cora will be my final guardian. When her time comes, I will give up the thread of my ninth life and live out whatever time I'm allowed on my own terms. After that, I would like to be buried with Cora so that I may accompany her into the Stardust Realm, and whatever adventures might come after this one."

A sharp inhale caught in the back of my throat.

Aunt Lavender frowned at her former familiar. "This is all a bit morbid, isn't it?"

"Hey, it worked for the Egyptian Pharaohs, and those guys worshiped cats, so clearly they knew what they were doing."

My vision swam as I bit back the tears that swelled at her declaration.

Selene looked up at me. "That is, if she'll have me."

I swallowed the lump in my throat and nodded. "It would be the honor of my lifetime, Selene."

Our gazes held for a long moment before she inclined her head in silent gratitude. When she lifted her face once more, the mischief had returned to her eyes. "Good," she declared, hopping down from her perch.

Mom and Aunt Lavender hung back as Selene sauntered toward the door of our hotel room, her tail aloft. Both women sniffled as they pulled me into a shared embrace.

When she reached the door, Selene turned back and flicked her tail. "Now, I don't care where we go to dinner, but it needs to have an outdoor patio so one of you can order me the biggest fish the chef can fit in a pan. All this decision making has me absolutely famished."

I sniffled and wiped at my eyes, eagerly nodding my agreement as our eyes met once more. "Only the best for my forever familiar."

Selene twitched her whiskers, her teeth flashing in a smile. "Well, if I'd known that would be your response, I'd have made up my mind months ago! What else can I get out of you? Hmm. What about a car? Something sleek and sporty. Checkers can work the pedals and I'll do the steering."

I burst out laughing. "Absolutely not!"

"Drats. That sure didn't last long." She swished her tail and turned back toward the door. "Oh well, the fish will have to do. But now I want two plates. I'm thinking something freshwater and something saltwater. Sort of a surf and surf deal."

I reached for my purse and smiled at Mom and Aunt Lavender. "We'd better hurry before she decides to order an entire aquarium as an appetizer."

"Hmm. An aquarium, huh? Now there's an idea."

"Not on your ninth life, cat!"

EPILOGUE

"Cora, we have a problem."

"Oh, gee. That's just what I wanted to hear tonight." I glanced over my shoulder as Selene sauntered into the kitchen, her tail aloft and her eyes wild. I paused my stirring and turned down the stove burner, letting the hot apple cider drop to an easy simmer.

"What did you do this time?" I asked, my voice flat. "Don't tell me you went and landed yourself on another neighborhood watch's most wanted list."

Selene scoffed and flicked her tail. "I was framed, and you know it!"

"Oh, is that right?" I leaned against the counter and planted a hand on my hip. "I saw the evidence, Selene. You shredded that clown into circus-colored confetti. All that was left were the rubber shoes and the little red nose, rolling down the sidewalk until it got caught in that sewer grate."

"Well, come on. Who decorates with life-size clown dolls?! I mean, honestly. The goddess should have struck them down for the mere idea."

My lips quirked to one side. "So, you're admitting it, then?"

"I'm not admitting anything."

"Oh, yes you are! You're afraid of clowns! After all these years we finally found your Achilles heel."

Selene's eyes went icy blue. "I do *not* have an Achilles heel, and I am *not* afraid of clowns. If anything, I'm allergic to tacky Halloween décor and was merely trying to avoid anaphylactic shock. There. You caught me. Are you happy now?"

She stuck her nose in the air.

I stifled a giggle and went back to stirring the cider. The batch smelled divine. My candle fragrances got pretty close, but there was just something extra magical about a pot of warm cider, simmering atop the stove on a cold, rainy autumn day.

"Okay. So, if it isn't the neighborhood watch on your tail, what gives? What's the big emergency? And if you ate the Halloween candy again, I'm going to cut off your fish allowance until New Year's."

Selene muttered something dark under her breath.

"What was that?" I asked, pitching my voice into a tone almost as sweet as the bag of chocolate-bathed nougat she'd gorged herself on over the weekend, leading to an after-hours visit with Dr. Kiki and her staff at the vet clinic.

"Will you just listen to me?!" she snapped.

I sighed and let the smile slide from my face. It was All Hallow's Eve and Clint and I (and by proxy, Selene) were throwing a Halloween bash for our friends and family. The candy bowls were stocked, spooky tea towels hung from the handles of the fridge and stove, and little felt ghosts were strung on a lanyard across the mantle. Of course, the real star of the show would be my haunted house candle, but I'd put off lighting it and activating the illusion until the first group of guests pulled into the drive.

"All right, fine," I said, lifting the spoon from the cider. "What's up?"

She paused and glanced over her shoulder, like something other than her shadow might be following her. Pippin was on a run with Clint, in an attempt to burn off some of the eager dog's energy before the kids arrived. He was good with kids, but there was always a risk of him accidentally knocking them over if he got too excited. So, if not the dog, what was she looking for?

I turned off the stove.

If Selene was nervous, that meant brace for the impending apocalypse.

"Well ... uh, you know how you wanted me to make some scary decorations for the trick-or-treaters?"

I cocked an eyebrow. "That's not quite the way I

remember it. You swiped my credit card and went on a shopping spree, aided and abetted by Checkers and that goddess-cursed AI shopping app on Clint's phone."

"You told me I should lend a paw! This is me, participating. Sheesh, damned if you do, damned if you don't with this one."

I folded my arms. "What did you do?"

"Fine, I might have used a little animation spell. Just a tiny dash of magic. I thought it would be fun if the cyclops dummy chased after the kids—"

"Selene!"

"What?"

Before I could offer further chastising, a loud *thunk* reverberated through the wall the kitchen shared with the garage. My eyes went wide. "Selene...?"

"Right. So ... like I was saying, the spell packed a little more punch than I intended and now there's a not-zero chance we have a cyclops-shaped golem in the garage."

Another *thump* sounded, the vibration loud enough to rattle the contents of the cupboards.

"Sweet Merlin's beard! Selene!"

"Don't get your granny panties in a bunch! I have a plan. All you have to do is cast a little wind spell and hold it still long enough for me to blast it into smithereens," she said, already heading toward the door to the garage. "Easy-peasy-lemon-squeezy."

A *crash* rattled my eardrums as what sounded like

the contents of Clint's tool chests crashed to the ground.

I rolled my eyes. "Right. Of course. Silly me for panicking."

"Come on," Selene said. "We need to hurry. I think it's getting hungry."

"Just perfect."

I yanked open the door to the garage, Selene hot on my heels. The scene that greeted us was pure chaos. The five-foot-tall rubber cyclops, now very much alive and very much enraged, was stomping around the garage, knocking over everything in its path. Wrenches and screwdrivers and a power drill lay scattered and Clint's carefully organized workbench stood in shambles.

"Oh, for the love of—Selene!" I shouted, ducking as a wrench flew past my head.

"Less scolding, more magicking!" Selene yelled back, darting between the cyclops's legs.

I focused my energy, summoning a gust of wind to push the creature back. It stumbled but didn't fall, its single eye glaring at me with rubber malevolence.

"Okay, new plan," I muttered. "Selene, can you distract it?"

"On it!" Selene called, then started yowling and dancing around the cyclops's feet. "Hey, ugly! Down here! Bet you can't catch me! Hey, Cora, should I tell it my name is Nobody?"

"Not the time, Selene," I replied through gritted teeth.

As the cyclops turned to swat at Selene, I concentrated harder, channeling my wind magic into a powerful vortex. The air swirled around the creature, lifting it off its feet and pinning it against the wall.

"Go, Selene!" I shouted, straining to hold the magic in place.

A burst of pink light streaked across the garage like the tail of a comet and hit the rubber cyclops in the eye. Of course she'd seen that as her bullseye. At first, nothing happened, but then, with a sound like a deflating balloon, the creature slumped in on itself until it was nothing more than a harmless rubber decoration once again.

I retracted my wind spell, and the dummy collapsed to the floor with a soft thud. We stood there for a moment, catching our breath and surveying the mess around us. With a sigh, I wiped the sheen of sweat from my brow and skewered Selene with a sidelong glare. "You're going to be the death of me."

She followed me as I returned to the kitchen. The mess in the garage would have to be dealt with later.

"Technically speaking, I have more incentive than anyone else to keep you in the land of the living," she reminded me as she strolled across the room.

"Right, right." I shook my head, dismissing my statement. "Okay, new house rule—no creating golems in the garage. I think that's pretty fair, don't you?"

Selene's eyes narrowed, but before she could argue the front door opened and the sound of frantic dog nails skidding across the hardwood sent her scampering for higher ground.

I grinned as Pippin burst into the kitchen, his tongue lolling and eyes soft. "Hey, baby boy! How was your run? Did Dad let you chase the squirrels and crows?"

Clint grinned as he wandered down the hall toward us.

Selene made a hacking sound from her perch on the back of the couch. "Honestly, Cora. If you engage in this level of baby talk with the dog, I shudder to think of how bad it will be with that spawn you're incubating—"

I bolted to my full height, fast enough to make my head swim. Across from me, Clint stopped dead in his tracks, his water bottle paused halfway to his lips. His eyes darted from me to Selene and back again. "Did she just—"

"Wait—what did you say?"

Selene swished her tail and eyed us. "What? Was it supposed to be a surprise?"

"Selene, I'm not—I'm not pregnant. And if this is some kind of sick crack about my jeans getting a little tighter, you can just take a long walk off a short pier!"

Selene scoffed. "Not pregnant? Okay, Cora. I'll play along."

Clint set his water bottle down and hurried across the kitchen. "Cora? What's going on?"

"I don't—" I frowned. There was a tiny chance, but no. She couldn't possibly know something like that.

"We're bonded, Cora. I can tell there's an extra little soul in there, soaking up some of the magic for itself. I first realized it on the island. You know, that's probably why the whole golem thing happened. Pregnancy does weird things to magic."

Clint blinked. "Golem? As in—"

"Yeah, it was a whole thing. She tried to bring the rubber cyclops to life, and then has the nerve to berate the neighbors for their clown." I paused and shook my head, clearing my mind. "Wait, are you serious, Selene? This isn't some kind of prank?"

She flopped onto her side and gave a dramatic roll of her eyes. "Go and pee on a stick if you don't believe me!"

A tiny twist of a smile bloomed on Clint's lips as he took my hands. "If there's one thing I know about Selene after all this time, it's that she has an often infuriating habit of being right."

"Thank you," she called from her perch.

I exhaled slowly and nodded. "I suppose there's only one way to find out."

ONE MAD-DASH TRIP to the pharmacy and three digital pregnancy tests later, we had our definitive answer, staring back at us with pixelated clarity.

PREGNANT

"I—I can't believe this is real!" I breathed, snuggled up against Clint's chest as he held me close. He hadn't let me go since I laid down the third test, likely to prevent me from taking a fourth.

Clint chuckled and I melted into the warmth of the sound and the way it felt to be in his arms. Our entire world had shifted right under our feet, and yet, there he was, as stable and unshakable as a block of granite.

Selene poked her head around the corner of the bathroom. "Don't you two have something to tell me?"

With eyes full of wonder and a few unshed tears, I grabbed the test and held it out, grinning. "We're having a baby!"

"Yes, yes, I *know*. You're supposed to tell me I was right!"

I laughed and placed the test back on the counter. "Fine, Selene, you were right."

She lifted her chin. "As always. Now, I have a little something for you."

Suspicion rolled across Clint's face as he looked from the cat to me. "It's never good when she has a surprise for us."

I gave a slight shake of my head, but it was too late, Selene was already gone.

She returned a minute later, levitating a slim gift box wrapped in sparkly pink wrapping paper over her head, as though it were a helium balloon on a string.

"What's this?" I asked, stepping toward her.

"A baby grand piano," she replied, tone thick with sarcasm. "The spawn is already soaking up your magic, don't tell me it's eating your brains, too. I don't want to have to have you committed, Cora, but I will, if it's the only way to keep you safe. A nice padded room, with no sharp corners, and a cozy little jacket, just for you."

With a frown, I yanked the gift box from the puff of magic. "Knock it off, Selene."

"It's a gift for the spawn," she replied as I started tugging the bow from the top of the package.

I paused. "Okay, let's nix the word *spawn* from your vocab. We already went over this when Cheyanne was pregnant with Pierce. Spawn isn't a nice word, Selene."

She shifted a glance at the unwrapped box. "Hmm. I might need to rethink the present then..."

"What?" When she didn't reply, I hurried to tear off

the paper. Clint took it from me, and I lifted the lid to reveal a baby onesie laid out flat. It was a pale purple color with black lettering, embellished with glittery fabric paint.

Clint choked as I read the front: "Selene's #1 Minion."

I burst out laughing.

IN THE AFTERMATH of our news, the tone of the party shifted slightly, but we managed to play it cool until the family arrived. Aunt Lavender and Checkers showed up as Sherlock and Watson, with Checkers in the fabled detective's hat. Cheyanne came as the Wicked Witch of the West, with Ruby and Emme and Pierce serving as her dutiful flying monkeys, while Evan played the part of the Scarecrow. Mom wore a red-and-white striped shirt and a pair of glasses with thick black frames. She'd come straight from a story hour at the library, where she'd introduced the kids to Waldo.

Leanna was on her way, but running a bit late, having been roped into supervising the Harvest Party at the academy where she worked.

With everyone gathered, Clint and I made our announcement, using Selene's gifted onesie as a prop.

Predictably, Mom burst into tears while everyone cheered, and crushed me in an embrace until Clint intervened and gently peeled me away.

"So, wait, was this planned?" Mom asked, still gripping my hands so tightly I thought I might lose circulation in my fingertips.

I craned around to look up at Clint. "Yes and no."

He laughed. "I would say mostly yes, but we didn't expect it to happen right off the bat."

"I was so busy in those weeks before the trip, with trying to get the shop ready for Halloween and planning to leave for Greece. I guess I didn't even realize I'd missed a cycle."

Mom squealed and pulled me in for another hug. "I'm so thrilled for you, honey—" Then, extending the hug to envelope Clint as well, she added, "For you both!"

"You're going to be awesome parents," Evan chimed in.

Fresh tears brimmed in my eyes. "Thanks, Ev."

"And you're sure it's a girl?" Cheyanne asked.

"That's what Selene said."

"Hence the purple onesie," Selene added helpfully. "It's a sixth sense."

"Wait, you said you knew about this since the island?" I asked, only just making the connection. A memory flashed back to me, of the two of us sitting on the shore, watching the moonlit sea. "And you knew it was a girl? Does that change your mind about ... you know? You could be my daughter's familiar."

Emme and Ruby were across the room, jumping on the sofa while Pierce chased after them. Likely the result of the sugar cookies and peanut butter cups they'd already eaten.

"I knew," Selene confirmed. "And no, it doesn't change anything. I've made up my mind."

The doorbell rang and Pippin barked. Cheyanne volunteered to go answer it, and came back with Leanna, who wore a stunning off-the-shoulder golden ball gown and long opera gloves, her hair swept back into a complicated twist of an updo.

She spotted the baby onesie as swiftly as an eagle sighting a plump field mouse, and the squealing and gushing and hugging started all over again.

Eventually, the party got off to a proper start, as the special candle I'd made was lit and the living room was transformed into a haunted house with cobwebs and creaky old furnishings and the kind of paintings where the eyes followed you. Clint turned on his carefully crafted playlist, I fired up the cider, and the first trick-or-treaters arrived.

Thankfully, Selene behaved herself for the most part, and did not attempt any further animation spells. Instead, she took a more old school approach of slinking around in the shadows and popping out to take a swipe at the kids' ankles as they left with their sugary loot.

Leanna's beau, Callum, arrived later in the evening, wearing a Beast costume that matched Leanna's Belle to movie-set-quality perfection. "It makes more sense now that I'm with you," he said to Leanna as she complimented the blue suit. "Half the bar patrons thought I was some kind of werewolf."

I snorted. "A little overdressed for a werewolf, I'd think."

Callum chuckled. "That's what I said!"

We made candy apples and carved pumpkins. Evan and Cheyanne left for an hour in the middle, to take the kids around our neighborhood to trick-or-treat, but returned in time to sit around the firepit, making s'mores and telling a few silly ghost stories, until Pierce crashed out in Evan's arms, and they decided to head home.

After everyone had gone, Clint and I snuggled up on the couch with the last of the cider, watching as the flame from my candle finally sputtered and died. The illusion broke and our living room was restored to its normal look, sans twisting shadows and tattered furniture. I turned my head on his shoulder and smiled up at him. "I guess next year's party will look a little different, huh?"

He brushed a kiss to my forehead. "I imagine it will. We'll be wildly sleep deprived, for one thing."

I laughed. "True. But think of the cute baby costume potential!"

Clint chuckled. "You think Selene is right, and that we're having a girl?"

I placed a hand over my stomach, which felt somehow different now.

"How is that a real question?" Selene asked, reappearing in the doorway. She glanced around, then called down the hall. "It's safe again, you big, whiny baby."

Pippin's nails clicked on the floor until he poked his head into the room, emitting a soft whine as he checked the corners for lingering shadows. The poor thing hadn't agreed with the Halloween candle.

Satisfied it was safe once more, he wagged his fluffy tail and trotted across the room. I stroked a hand over his silky fur and he jumped up onto the couch beside me.

"Some guard dog," Selene scoffed. She hopped up into one of the overstuffed chairs opposite the couch and flicked her tail toward the remote control and sent it levitating toward me. "Come on. I want to watch *Hocus Pocus* one more time before we bid this holiday goodbye."

I laughed and turned on the TV. "You just like it because there's a cat."

"Naturally," she purred. "Although, I also relate to Winifred."

"Ah." I grinned and found the movie. The opening credits began to play and I set the remote down. "Well, you'll have to get over the whole allergy to children thing in, what, seven and a half months?" I added, settling back into Clint's side.

She swished her tail. "Cora, you know how I feel about talking during movies."

Clint smiled down at me. "A lot may change before next Halloween, but I think it's safe to say, one thing, at least, will never change."

I looked over at my familiar's profile and smiled. "I'm good with that."

THE END

A note from Selene:

So, we've reached the end of the story. And I get it. You're sad. Who could blame you? I'm the best! Who *wouldn't* want to read more about all of my fabulous adventures?

Well, I suppose if I've learned anything from my time with Cora, it's that all things must eventually come to an end. It's just the way this whole *life* gig works. A clear oversight, if you ask me, but hey, I don't make the rules.

And believe me, I've tried.

Now, come on, chin up. Don't go getting this book all soggy and ruin my gorgeous portrait on the cover.

Purr-haps we will meet again someday.

Until then, look for the magic in the world around

you. It's there. And remember, don't tempt fate (or any of The Fates, turns out they're the type to hold a grudge).

Oh, and if you see a cat, give them a fish. It's the right thing to do.

~Selene

ALSO BY DANIELLE GARRETT

One town. Two spunky leading ladies.
More magic than you can shake a wand at.
Welcome to Beechwood Harbor.

Come join the fun in Beechwood Harbor, the little town where witches, shifters, ghosts, and vamps all live, work, play, and— mostly—get along!

The two main series set in this world are the Beechwood Harbor Magic Mysteries and the Beechwood Harbor Ghost Mysteries.

In the following pages you will find more information about those books, as well as my other works available.

Alternatively, you can find a complete reading list on my website:

www.DanielleGarrettBooks.com

In Winterspell Lake there are things darker than midnight...

Sprinkles and Sea Serpents is the first book in a brand new paranormal cozy mystery series by Danielle Garrett. This series features magic, mystery, family squabbles, sassy heroines, and a mysterious monster hunter—all with a little sugar sprinkled on top.

Find the Sugar Shack Witch Mysteries on Amazon.

ABOUT THE AUTHOR

Danielle Garrett has been an avid bookworm for as long as she can remember, immersing herself in the magic of far-off places and the rich lives of witches, wizards, princesses, elves, and some wonderful everyday heroes as well. Her love of reading naturally blossomed into a passion for storytelling, and today, she's living the dream she's nurtured since the second grade—crafting her own worlds and characters as an author.

A proud Oregonian, Danielle loves to travel but always finds her way back to the Pacific Northwest, where she shares her life with her husband and their beloved menagerie of animal companions.

Visit Danielle today at her website or say "hello" on Facebook.

www.DanielleGarrettBooks.com